DIVE

DIVE

a novel

Bradford Middleton

NEW PULP PRESS

Published by New Pulp Press, LLC, 926 Truman Avenue, Key West, Florida 33040, USA.

For information contact:
Publisher@NewPulpPress.com

ISBN-13: 978-0692565599 (New Pulp Press)
ISBN-10: 0692565590

DIVE

ONE

Saturday mornings generally meant that Jack Thompson would wake late, usually in a state of delirium after a Friday night of heroic drinking. He would have hoped to have exorcised all the demons that had built up in him during his week at work at the university. His Friday nights had become a ritual, part of a routine that Jack saw as necessary in order to live as good a life as possible, one that was both tolerable and occasionally enjoyable. It would start at the bar nearest work where he would occasionally be joined by a colleague or two before setting home with a take-away on the train and the delights of his local pub mere yards from his front door. It was close enough to stagger home from no matter how drunk he had got and he invariably got very drunk. It also helped that there was a small shop in between as well that at weekends sold alcohol until deep in to the night.

This particular morning it was clear that Jack had enjoyed a pretty crazed night; there were beer cans and a bottle of whisky, all empty, sprawled over his living room floor. What came as even more of a shock was Jack waking on his armchair in his living room. His head was pounding and his gut felt terrible. Climbing out of his chair he caught a glimpse of himself in a mirror; even he thought he looked bad. The night before they, whoever they were, had stayed up late, very, very late indeed and judging by the ash-tray a small forest of weed had been enjoyed too. It was inevitable that a woman would have had to be involved; Jack knew it was only on those rare occasions that him and his bunch of loser, middle-aged friends were enjoying the company of women that they ever ended up in the kind of situation that had clearly developed on this particular Friday night. Jack struggled through the debris to his kitchen where he knew he would either be sick in his sink or he would get a mug of tea. He felt his gut and knew that it would be OK to eat so he prepared a couple of slices of toast and his mug of tea. This was all part of the routine that was his life.

Jack often found that routine ruled his life; work was the same time everyday and his weekends generally followed a similar pattern. Saturdays were often the happiest time of his week as he had no work to go to, no one to see until he was ready and most importantly he got to smoke as much weed as he wanted. It was all a part of the routine that was his life and the reason his flat was his favourite place, even more so than his local pub.

His flat wasn't much but it was better than any of the other places he had lived in since leaving home some twenty years before. It was a simple space, divided in to two rooms. His main living room was at the back with a pretty pleasant view of the garden and then there was the 'weird' one, being that it encapsulated his bedroom and kitchen with no natural light. It was always this room that people always seemed to comment on whenever they visited. He had always lived in places like this; they were the only kind of place he could afford and over the years he had grown used to the limited space and the problems that came with sharing a bath room with fifteen other flats.

Jack didn't mind being unhygienic as it limited his experience of having to deal with other people. He had never really been a people person and a life of isolation suited him. Even at work it had ceased being a problem; Jack was merely the strange working-class guy who seemed a bit shy and very occasionally smelt a bit fruity.

His living room was packed of shelving units full of books, records, CDs and films and in the little bit of space that was left there was just enough room for him to fit a two-seater sofa, an armchair and his dilapidated record player and TV set-up. It was regularly full of debris from his recreational pursuits; an over loaded ash tray that suggested he didn't have long for this life as well as various empty bottles or cans if it had been one of those nights. He smoke and drank most days but still felt he had it under control to the degree that he wasn't supporting a habit; he rarely got either very stoned or very drunk, he merely liked ticking over. If it didn't become habitual he felt he was doing OK; there were times he over-did it on both counts but fortunately for his sanity and his money it was rare, at most twice a week. Now whilst that might sound quite excessive but it was a great improvement on the four or five times that he had subjected himself to during his teenage and twenty-something years. It was all about the ticking over, maintaining the routine that he had grown used too.

It then became clear what was going to happen that day; he would finish his breakfast of tea, toast and joint before clearing up all the debris from the night before. After that it was often time for the football coverage. Jack loved football, it was one of the things he shared with the masses, but his team always came as a shock to people when he told them.

"I'm a Millwall supporter," he would tell whoever and they would look at him in shock as if he had just eaten a baby for breakfast. It was something he had got used to; now almost forty-years old he had enjoyed the inevitable shock of the hundreds of people he had ever talked to about football. Unfortunately he rarely had the money to attend games but he had little interest in doing what the rest of the country did on that day either; namely shop. He'd only ever enjoyed shopping for books, music and films that was enough for him; clothes to him were just something to keep him warm, he'd never cared about labels or fashions and with his jobs even if he had he could never have afforded such luxuries; Jack's priorities lie elsewhere. During the summer months, when there was no football, he would occasionally end up in the pub in the afternoon with his group of weird friends and he could witness the full-blown consumerist frenzy from closer quarters. It was a terrifying scene. He would spend his time in the pub with the same group of weird, dysfunctional people who had over time become a very close-knit group of friends. They were his people and whilst not having much in common with any of them anymore he could at least trust them not to mess with his mind. After years of leading the kind of life Jack had chosen to follow he found himself pretty close to the edge a lot more than the average thirty-nine year old would.

Private time on a Saturday was one of the highlights of his week; away from the stupidity of most people and a time to just completely switch off. It was a time to forget everything; work, despite being at one of the top colleges of the University of London, often meant dealing with some of the most socially inept, publically schooled Home Counties types he had ever had the misfortune to have to deal with. They were the polar opposite of Jack and somehow their stupidity always seemed to demean Jack even further in their eyes. It was one of the reasons he preferred keeping himself isolated at work. Outside of a small group of people who he shared office space with he was generally ignored and that suited him.

***

Jack had been born in 1971, a time that signaled the end of the hippy dream and heralded the birth of a new forgotten generation that was to undergo turmoil and hostility at every turn. It had been made clear to him at school that he would never progress in life. He was being prepared for a life on the poverty line, simply another drone that would be used to support the system that would keep him impoverished. His future was to be one of low-cost slum housing with no real chance to truly excel at anything. These were simply the type of things he was expected to get used to and deal with. At primary school he'd had his milk taken from him by some tin-pot dictator in government and at secondary level, despite being one of the brighter students, was told to not even bother thinking about university as it was made clear it wasn't for people like him. When he heard that George, a friend who somehow got a place at Oxford, was driven to suicide inside his first eighteen months it made him angrier than he had ever been and even more determined to prove them all wrong. After gaining a place at a small former polytechnic in southeast London he took the opportunity with both hands and never looked back until four years later he'd finally decided to end his higher education experience when he successfully passed a Masters degree in a northern town. This was the only time that Jack had lived outside of south London and it had been a real eye-opener; how different life was up there. It was a weird, invigorating and glorious year that he lived there and it didn't matter that what he studied would eventually prove pointless. Unfortunately all the jobs he thought he could do were in London so he had no choice but to return and he subsequently got a job at the University of London in a lowly admin role. He'd now been there for nearly ten years and despite still being relatively happy in his position it wasn't what he had hoped for. It didn't matter that he was overlooked every time a possible promotion was up for grabs; they inevitably bought in some new kid who'd previously studied at the institute. A dropout who simply couldn't deal with life in the real world, a world far removed from their public school background. At least, he thought, he had enough money to live the kind of life he wanted – a small bedsit which was crammed full of records, books and DVD's and enough money to get drunk or high every weekend was all he really needed.

He accepted the fact that he was stuck in a rut but it was a rut he had grown fond of and with his fortieth birthday in the not too distant future he was relatively happy with his position in life. All that was really missing, he occasionally thought, was a woman to spend his time with; all his most recent conquests had been women of a certain mental disposition. They had a tendency towards insanity; they all appeared to be completely mad. It was often this kind that felt attracted to Jack and his friends; it was a rare occurrence that any of them had a chance to meet a woman but the ones they did they always seemed to be mad. It had been like that for a long time now and it appeared it would remain this way.

This afternoon however was developing nicely. His hangover had transpired not to have been as bad as he envisaged and now with the time approaching three o'clock and the start of the football season the skies had opened and rain poured down to devour the city. Millwall were playing away to Blackpool that day so the weather wouldn't affect them; it just meant the people he despised would get soaked. This pleased him greatly as the rain cleansed the streets of all the dirt and mess that had been left in that day's consumerist onslaught. The rain washed away used fast food wrappers and paper bags turned to tatters the second they came in to contact with the elements.

He turned his TV set on and found a random sports news station that would keep him company for the next couple of hours and keep him updated on how Millwall were doing. He made another mug of tea and rolled a joint. This was always his favourite time of the week unless of course his team lost which had so often been the case over the course of his life.

Sitting in his armchair, the same place he had slept that morning, he smoked joint after joint that soon had him grinning like a chimpanzee until it hit him; the wonderful realisation that Millwall had indeed won, a fluky 1-0 victory with a late goal after being largely played off the park for nearly eighty minutes. The news of the result had left him feeling pretty delirious and he decided it was time for some loud music. Loud music never came any better than the greatest rock 'n' roll record of all-time, Funhouse by The Stooges. As it roared in to action with Iggy shouting about being 'down on the street' Jack leapt from his armchair and punched the air, happy that his team had won and at last it was Saturday evening. The smoke, the music and the probability that later that evening he would be drunk all came together like an unholy trinity, a glorious moment of oh so rare bliss.

Jack knew it was time for some early dinner as he needed to get out to the pub. There were never any arrangements made for Saturday night; it was just assumed that the group of friends would meet in the local pub. Jack would meet up with his bunch of weird mates and a huge quantity of alcohol would be consumed. It never really seemed to matter when he arrived there was always someone there he would know and soon enough all of the main characters would be in situ doing what they loved the most.

TWO

It became immediately apparent that it wasn't going to be a regular Saturday night as one of the first things he saw upon exiting the communal front door was an old drunk falling over on the other side of his street. It was a character he knew well, he generally saw him slumped on the bench outside the Post Office with a huge bottle of extra strength white cider for company. It was however unusual to see him off the high street and Jack decided it was just best to let the weed take control, taking him back to his calm peaceful place, and begin his walk to the pub.

'That could have been me,' Jack thought to himself, briefly remembering the time after finishing university when he very nearly became one of the homeless masses on the streets of London.

Jack's meditation was broken by a scream emanating from the other side of the street; the old man had clearly fallen over but Jack knew what he needed to do; he merely continued on his path to the pub. The old man was a regular sight in the neighbourhood, always in his long trench coat no matter what the weather, but this time it appeared he had somehow lost his trousers. Jack turned the corner and it was now only a short walk up the hill before he got to the pub but the next thing he heard was an even more horrendous scream. This time however it was closer and as Jack turned he couldn't believe what he was seeing. The old man was running, straight for him, with his jacket open showing off his wrinkled and highly abused body, lithe stomach muscles and a pair of boxer shorts barely in one piece. Jack knew he was in imminent danger of attack and he began to walk much faster. It wasn't long before the old man caught him up.

"Mate ..." his voice pleaded in pathetic tones; Jack simply ignored him, hoping that he would go away. As he carried on walking he hoped the atypical London response would be enough to persuade the derelict to leave him alone.

"Please ... can you spare some change?" the voice pleaded again.

"I been beaten up, they stole my trousers the bastards ... I got nothing." Turning the corner at last Jack could now see the pub and knew that his ordeal would soon be over. However it quickly became apparent that it wasn't going to be as easy as simply ignoring him. This guy would not get bored with the chase so desperate were his circumstances. The old guy kept pace with Jack all the way to the entrance to the bar. It was then that disaster struck.

"Sorry mate but you two can't come in here. Not dressed like that."

"What?" came Jack's immediate response, "You don't get it ... he ain't with me, he's just trying to get some money off me to buy some new trousers. I'm meant to be meeting some friends inside."

"Not tonight mate, not with your mate. You just aren't the type of people we want drinking here."

"Don't you understand he's not with me," Jack pleaded growing increasingly desperate.

"Too bad for you I don't care. Get out of my pub before

it turns in to trouble. You get it?"

Jack got it alright but who the hell was this guy; he'd been drinking at this pub for nearly a decade and he'd never seen him before. He looked at his reflection in the door and it shocked him; he shared some characteristics with his homeless assailant, bad hair, bad teeth, bad grooming.

Turning to the old man Jack asked him what it would take for him to leave him alone. He was feed up, not being allowed in the pub was a disaster; he decided to call his best mate Frank who he could see sitting at their usual table at the back starting on what looked like a lovely pint of Guinness. Taking his phone from his jacket pocket he turned and realised the old man hadn't gone away and was now instead looking with deranged eyes at Jack's phone. It was like a piece of technology from a science-fiction movie that he'd never seen before.

Jack began to walk away from the situation but as his phone reached his ear he felt it being tugged away by a hand that wasn't his. The old man had clawed it from his palm and immediately began running.

'Can tonight get any worse?' Jack thought to himself as he gave chase. Looking up he saw the old man running down the street towards what looked like a gang of old homeless men. Pausing momentarily Jack briefly contemplated his next move; looking down the street he could see the man who had suddenly become his arch nemesis gesticulating excitedly at his latest acquisition. With the realisation that he could not live without all the information stored on his phone Jack knew he now had to take some action.

"Hey ..." Jack shouted at them as he walked over to confront the group, "give me back my phone and nothing bad will happen you get it?"

This was greeted with complete silence by the gang in front of him and he walked to the centre of the group to confront his newfound enemy. A shove in his back pushed him in to the thief and Jack seized the opportunity to grab his phone before suddenly feeling a harsh whack on the back of his head. He fell to the ground but retained a tight grip on the phone, slowly struggling to his feet. It was at this point he realised all the men surrounded him were big, bigger than him anyway which took some doing. At six feet tall Jack had never considered himself to be short until this moment. All six of the men looked as if they could have been former military. He immediately became scared of the situation in which he now found himself. Still clutching the phone but with a deluge of rain now falling from the sky it became apparent that Jack should probably just go home and re-group. One of the refuseniks suddenly realised what was happening and just how much cheap alcohol the gang could buy with money made from selling the phone. He threw himself at Jack who again fell to the ground. That last joint had clearly been a little bit too strong and it was then that things got even stranger. The rain stopped instantly as if by remote control and suddenly a bright white light focused in on the group who were triumphantly looking at his mobile phone. However in the blink of an eye they were gone and what appeared to be a flying saucer was moving off in to the night sky. It appeared the group and, more importantly for Jack, his phone had gone.

It was indeed an unusual Saturday as there wasn't anyone around who could explain what had just happened. Jack realised that barring any Fox Mulder type heroics he was to be phoneless until Monday when he could go to the shop and buy a new one.

"How am I going to tell Frank and the guys that I'm not going to make it to the pub tonight?" he said to no one in particular, his spirit finally crushed.

As he walked past the bar he took in the fearsome eyes of the barman ensuring he was indeed walking past. Jack was confused; what exactly had just happened. Had aliens just hijacked his phone along with a group of random homeless alcoholics or was that joint just really, really strong? It had to have happened just as he remembered it because he felt his knee hurt from where he had fallen over and the fact that his phone and the gang had disappeared. Fortunately the journey back to his house was easier; he shook his head in disbelief at what had happened to his night out. He knew that once back in the flat he would have to smoke a really strong joint, quite possibly several very strong ones. He would listen to the first album by the Pink Floyd. Piper at the Gates of Dawn was always a great album to fry the brain too and tonight was definitely turning in to one of those nights when the brain needed frying.

About half way through the CD Jack remembered seeing some flyers in the hallway for a pub under new management. It promised cheap drinks and who knew what else? As the album came to a close with the enchanting Bike Jack knew that nothing could freak him out now. Not after what he'd already seen tonight and not after the magic of the weed and the mad genius of the Pink Floyd.

Despite this he did keep checking en route to this new pub for the group who had stolen his phone; he wondered when they would be back from their intergalactic adventures. Turning on to the high street, about two hundred metres up from his local pub, he saw the pub he was actually going to. There wasn't even a member of staff on the door of this pub so Jack knew he was going to have no problem getting a beer. From the outside it looked like any normal pub and quite safe for a quiet drink or three before going home to watch the Football League Show on TV. After all he'd experienced he was quite happy to see the pub sparsely populated. There were mainly groups of young looking people gathered around the tables around the main bar. Jack was pleased to see that his favourite place, a stool at the bar, was open. Sitting down after taking his coat off and placing it on the back of his chair, he leant forward picking up a flyer. Deals on pints and shots, tonight might not be that quiet after all Jack thought. A young woman came over and looked at him like she'd just trodden in something unpleasant.

"Pint of the Old Ale and double Havana Club with ice" he asked her in his most polite tones.

"Seven-twenty that'll be," she said placing his drinks before him on the bar. He drank half the pint slowly whilst the ice melted in his rum; the rum went down in one and tasted truly delicious. The sweetest moment came though when he added some of the ale in to the mix. It was now time for a smoke. Leaving his coat and drink at the bar he moved outside and smoked his roll-up quickly. Walking back in to the bar he could feel a pair of eyes following his very path back to his seat. Jack knew not to take any notice of them; he'd already had too much trouble that night and in a situation like this his mind could think of nothing other than avoiding any more trouble.

THREE

Sitting back at the bar, he was desperately trying to get the attention of the bar staff as his beer was nearing the end and he needed a re-fill. It was then things got even weirder.

"Hi," a sexy female voice said, " ... would you mind if I got a roll-up from you. Can you spare one?"

"Sure thing love, that's not a problem," he found himself replying. It was rare for Jack to talk to women and it was almost unheard of for one to approach him. He then realised that she was only interested in the contents of his tobacco pouch, or at least that's what he thought. 'What else could she want?' he thought turning to face her. She was a beautiful young woman who Jack concluded was at least ten years younger than him.

"When I get back do you mind if I come and join you?"

"That's fine but I can't promise to be the best company, I've had an odd night to say the least."

As she walked off for her smoke Jack finally got the attention of the bar staff.

"An Old Ale and a double Havana Club over ice" he told the young barman with a smile developing across his face. As the drinks arrived the strange woman returned.

"Hi, I'm Clare" she announced pulling up a stool next to where Jack sat.

"My name's Jack. Care for a drink Clare?"

"Sure, if that's alright? I'll have a gin and tonic please."

"No problems."

The bar man came over quicker this time seeing that Jack was sat with a beautiful young woman. Jack ordered a gin and tonic, ice and lemon.

The drink came quickly and was cheap. Clare sat on her stool, sipping her drink through a straw. It was her who started the conversation; Jack's paranoia meant he was still convinced that this was all a prelude to a huge joke on him, that at any moment she would stop being so kind and pour the drink he had just bought her all over him causing her friends to point and laugh. Public humiliations were not uncommon for Jack; they had occurred throughout his life and they had always made his already paranoid outlook even more concentrated.

Once she finished her drink his mind began to wonder just what she was up to. He hadn't been with a woman for a long time and especially one as beautiful and young as Clare appeared to be.

'There must be something terribly wrong with her if she wants to sit here and chat to me; what a waste of a Saturday night.' This was Jack's paranoia speaking to him again; his recent misadventures with women had all ended in disaster as they either turned out to be completely crazy or just obsessed with the idea of getting married and other such grown-up worries.

"Care for a drink Jack?" she asked returning her empty glass to the bar. The young man rushed over again.

"Another gin and tonic with ice and lemon?" he asked.

"Yes please and a pint for my friend here. He drinks the Old Ale."

"Ah yes, the Old, a very nice strong beer," the guy

enthused as if he drank nothing else. Jack scowled at him knowing he was just saying that to impress Clare and that he had probably never even tasted the beer he was now eulogising. An hour in to the night the pair had not stopped talking; Jack occasionally paused to take in her beautiful vision. She was quite tall, maybe five-nine, slim but curvy with gorgeous natural red hair. The more he thought about her the more he convinced himself that she was just lonely and wanting some company for the evening; he knew that nothing could ever happen between them. He thought it was impossible but slowly, after many more beer and rum chasers, Jack was becoming convinced that maybe something could happen. He was drinking himself in to a newfound delirium of joyfulness.

"I know we've only been talking shit tonight Clare but I've had a really fun time with you" Jack declared just as the bell for last orders rang. He paused, unsure of how to proceed, before looking at her face just as she turned to face him.

"Yes," Clare said, setting him up for his fall.

"Well, would you consider continuing back to mine? A drink and a few joints sound good?" His courage had carried him through but what came next truly shocked him.

She leant over, kissing him on the lips, and said "Sure, that'd be nice I reckon. How about we get a decent bottle of gin from the corner-shop?"

"Great idea, let's get out of her" Jack said downing the remnants of his last pint almost in a state of disbelief at what he'd just heard himself say. Helping Clare in to her coat it became immediately apparent that a few people in the pub were as shocked as Jack was that the old man was leaving with the young beauty. He felt the unfamiliar feeling of smugness consume him as they left together. What an odd evening it had turned out to be; what an awfully odd evening and it wasn't even over yet. Seeing her standing he took in her sexy outfit; a tight plain white T-shirt with a brown cardigan over it, a medium length skirt and what appeared to be tights covered her legs. A pair of cool looking trainers finished off her outfit. As they walked out the pub, turning down the hill again but this time towards the corner-shop, Jack kept a sharp eye out for the refuseniks. The shop was just two doors up from the pub he had earlier been refused entry to and therefore near the scene of the earlier abduction. It had indeed been a very strange evening.

FOUR

Jack was well known to the guys who ran the corner-shop; it transpired he had been in there the night before with a whole party of people, buying whisky and beer. He'd been a customer of the shop throughout his ten-year residency around the corner and over the fullness of time had grown to appreciate their kindness. They would serve him whatever he wanted no matter how drunk he was as long as he had the money to buy it. Despite his desperate loneliness and his desire for female companionship he was also keen to not take advantage of any situation that may occur back at his flat; he didn't want to end up in bed with Clare unless it was something she really wanted. He was still sure that nothing was going to happen between them though.

"Evening guys, how's it going tonight?" Jack enquired of the young man behind the counter and his older brother stocking the shelves.

"Yeah, it's all good Jack and how are you doing?"

"Well tonight I'm doing just excellent. Me and my friend would like a small bottle of gin and a bottle of tonic water."

The young man leant down behind the counter and promptly re-appeared with a small bottle of Gordon's gin.

"Ah now, when I say small bottle, I don't mean that small ... just a seventy size will do."

"OK," the young assistant replied reaching down

slightly less than previously and pulled out a much bigger bottle of Gordon's.

"That's better; now what do we owe you?"

"Sixteen quid please Jack" the young assistant informed him. Jack felt Clare appear behind him, forcing a ten-pound note in to his hand.

"Thanks babe, much appreciated," he said offering her a couple of pound to make it even.

Jack and Clare turned to leave and suddenly Jack heard the furore the situation had caused amongst the staff.

"Was that really ...?"

"Yeah, what's a woman like that doing ...?"

Jack smiled broadly as they got back on the street.

"I'm just around the corner from here ... where do you live?"

"I share a house with some other women up near the train station. Elgin Close, you know it?"

"Sure I know it; I was born round this way and know everywhere. As you know though I did get to escape for a while but now I'm back and it looks like I'll never escape. I hope my tiny flat isn't too bad for you?" They were now approaching the house and Jack was suddenly worried about what he may find once they were inside. He hoped there were no porn magazines lying around. That would immediately create a bad first impression.

Walking up to the front door Jack reached in to the pocket of his coat to reach for his keys. The coat, a cheap leather job from Camden market bought only a few months before but already looking like it was old, was the last piece of clothing he had bought and that was only out of need in a time of emergency. He'd been to a party shortly before and had got so drunk on whisky that he blacked-out; the next thing he was aware of was waking up in bed still fully clothed but covered in blood. He had apparently fallen and broken his nose and his bed that morning looked like a piece of furniture from a low-budget horror movie.

"Well this is me," Jack fan-fared in his usual self-deprecating manner as they walked up the stairs to his large terraced block. The entry hall was a real mess with post lying around on the floor and empty recycling boxes taking up a lot of other space. The only one full was his, full of old newspapers as well as a myriad selection of wine, spirit and beer bottles.

"It ain't much is it? What do you think?" he asked.

"Well it's kind of like mine except our place is a bit tidier. I suppose that's what happens when you get three women together in a house ..."

Jack laughed, hoping that the rest of the house was either asleep, out somewhere or just not listening. Reaching his flat door Jack unlocked and suggested to Clare that he go in first; he just wanted to be certain that there was nothing lying around that would embarrass him. It all seemed fine and so Jack held the door open, allowing Clare entry.

"Shall I hang your coat up?" he asked.

"I think I can manage that thanks how about you just fix us up with a couple of drinks?"

"Sure thing," Jack announced walking off to the kitchen to grab a couple of glasses. He took the bottles with him and moments later returned carrying two rather strong gin and tonics. He suddenly realised that he was quite nervous, it had been some years since Jack had been in this position and he knew the drink would help calm him down. Placing the drinks down on a small stool he asked Clare if she wanted to listen to some music.

"Sure, what you got?"

"Well how about coming over here and checking it out?"

Clare was shocked at the size of Jack's vinyl collection; she hadn't seen someone with that much since leaving home. Her Dad had been a collector she told him but still she went through the first few before pulling out the wonderful Spiritualized album Ladies and Gentlemen We Are Floating In Space. Knowing what this album always did to him Jack took a sip of his drink before beginning to prepare a joint.

Gesticulating with his hands he asked Clare if she cared to help him smoke some.

"I thought you'd never ask," she replied, laughing as if she knew that by choosing that specific album it would lead to this situation. In all honesty it could have been any record she had chosen.

"Make sure it isn't too strong though, it's been a while since I smoked any of that!"

"No problem love, I use it only moderately now in comparison to the quantities I used to back in the day. I promise you though it will get you buzzing nicely."

He pulled out his rolling papers and constructed them in to the cone that they would smoke. As he began sprinkling the tobacco in to the joint he felt her head lean over and rest gently on his shoulder. Reaching the crucial stage of actual assemblage Clare kicked off her shoes and pulled her feet up on to the sofa. As he was about to complete the process he noticed her face turn to his and slowly, teasingly, her lips moved towards his neck where she kissed him, ever so gently. This surprised and pleased him but almost made him drop the contents of the paper. Once the construction was complete he turned to her and pulled her close; they kissed passionately for the first time and it felt like Jack's life would never be the same again.

With the joint lit and Clare concentrating on her gin and tonic Jack took a few tokes before passing it over to her. Reaching for his drink he felt completely at ease with the situation. Clare took a couple of tokes of the joint before turning her attention back to Jack. She admitted that she hadn't smoked weed for nearly a decade and on the last occasion she didn't enjoy herself.

"This one though, wow, it makes me feel really chilled and comfortable. I'm guessing the environment has something to do with that though. Now why did you really invite me back here, it wasn't just for a drink and a joint was it?"

"Well, honestly, it's been a while since I had an opportunity like this ..."

"What kind of opportunity you think you got tonight then?"

"Oh I didn't mean it like that ..."

"Sure," she replied inhaling deeply on the joint. She stood up and taking off her cardigan she passed the joint back to Jack.

"So, what do you think?" she asked.

"Well, you are definitely one of the most beautiful

women I've had the pleasure of talking to in a long time. I've always had a thing for natural redheaded women!" he confessed.

He lay back on his couch and took another deep toke on the joint. He couldn't quite believe what was happening as she began to move around his living room in time to the music. She was indeed a beautiful vision and as he continued to smoke the joint he couldn't take his eyes off her. She was twirling around before him and slowly began to remove her clothing.

'What is going on?' Jack thought to himself, in disbelief that here was a beautiful twenty-seven-year-old woman performing for him. He felt a rare twinge in his jeans as he became more turned on. She removed her skirt and her T-shirt and once he'd put the joint out she moved over towards him clad in only her tights, pants and bra. She looked astonishing; sexy and cool all at once. This was definitely the best night Jack had experienced for some years and he knew it was only going to get better when she began walking towards him.

"Why don't you undo your jeans for me," she instructed as she closed in on him. He took the opportunity to remove his trainers and socks too; he wouldn't want anyone to have to do that for him.

His erection grew even stiffer as she grabbed the legs of his jeans and pulled. They were off in a flash and she, somewhat teasingly, asked if it had been a while since someone had paid him this kind of attention.

"Well yeah it has, especially a specimen as fine as you. Wow you got me so hot already." As she removed her tights Jack felt his cock finally become fully erect and more turned-on that he could remember being in a long time.

She moved in and joined him on the couch, kissing him before whispering "Don't worry I'll be gentle." It reminded him of losing his virginity some twenty years before but this time he wasn't at all nervous. He felt comfortable with this woman who had only come in to his life some hours before. He reasoned that the vast quantity of weed and the alcohol he'd consumed had produced this state. He knew tonight was going to be different altogether from that disastrous night he lost his virginity. She crawled on top of him and pulled him close, kissing him passionately whilst allowing his hands to unclip her bra. She leant up and pulled it off revealing a beautifully pert pair of breasts that he was eager to familiarize himself with. With Jack now sat up she ripped his T-shirt off his torso. With them now down to just their boxers and panties respectively and with the foreplay having elicited the desired affect Jack grabbed hold of her, spinning her around and laying her down on the couch. He edged down over her stomach, kissing her all over before arriving at the top of her panties. He paused momentarily, trying to remember how he had last got a woman off using his cunnilingus technique, and taking the opportunity to kiss her again. She was a fantastic kisser and Jack knew that her body was his; he could do pretty much whatever he wanted from this point on. He went back down and removed her panties to reveal a slightly stubbly pussy. He kissed at the lips now and he could feel her quiver; it was a magical moment. He moved a couple of fingers up in to her passage whilst still kissing around her lips.

"Oh my god," she responded, "that feels so fucking good!"

"How about I replace my fingers with what you really want?" he retorted.

"Mmmm, yes please" she said whilst grabbing at his boxers and freeing him of any last piece of modesty. She was as excellent a fuck as she looked as if she would be; she pounded his cock into orgasm before becoming overwhelmed herself. He felt her pussy tighten around his cock and knew he'd got her off. Her face and reaction suggested that she had enjoyed herself too and that indeed it had been a while since she had enjoyed herself so much.

Collapsing back on to the couch with a broad smile across her face Jack knew exactly what was needed. He rolled over, grabbed his tin and tobacco and began to build another joint. This time however it was stronger than the last one; he was spent for the night and all he wanted now was to lie with her and bask in the glory of the huge orgasm that had swept through them both. After taking a couple of fairly big tokes on the joint he passed it over to Clare and, after only a couple, she rolled over and began to doze off. It had indeed been a very strange night and who knew where it would go from here.

FIVE

That morning Jack's first instinct upon waking was to look over at Clare; check that she was indeed real and that what happened last night did really happen. He knew what he needed, a good mug of tea and a roll-up. It was another of his rituals; every day when hung-over or stoned from the night before he would go through this now much played-out routine. He would fill the saucepan with enough water for a few and he would then throw in a tea bag, a whole heap of sugar and a lot of milk. If there was one thing about this ritual that he hated it was the hangover that inevitably accompanied it. The tea always helped though, rehydrating his poor body and making him feel slightly more like a member of the human race.

After about thirty seconds his gaze averted from Clare's gorgeous face and body towards his tobacco pouch. He reached for a paper as he climbed from his bed intent on getting to the kitchen to brew the tea; he thought he make more than normal seeing as he had company. The water began to boil a few minutes later and Jack completed his rituals. His roll-up was firmly in place and his tea was ready to drink. Entering his living room again he became immediately aware of Clare moving and stretching herself awake.

"Wow," Jack muttered as he took in the sight of her gorgeously pert breasts. The thing he liked about her most was her teeth; they were not perfect but for some reason they suggested a ravishingly sexy individual as they had a gap between the two front teeth. It was definitely a noticeable gap and last night as her mouth took his cock he could feel the gap; it made him tingle.

"What?"

"Oh nothing sweet, fancy some tea? I recommend milk and sugar with what I can offer I'm afraid."

"Sure but not too much sugar, maybe a small one."

With the water recently boiled it didn't take long to make Clare a decent mug of tea but by the time he walked back in she was sat on the couch in one of his old punk-rock shirts. It was long enough on her, despite her not immodest height, to almost work as a skirt. A pretty short skirt Jack was pleased to notice.

"Oh hey, I thought you'd still be in bed ..." he stated rather obliquely upon entering his living room.

"Don't worry; I'm not in a rush to get anywhere today. I can stay for as long as I want to and right now there ain't anywhere else I'd rather be than here with you. Sound good?"

"Sounds like a great plan baby."

It was clear that she had expected to wake up here; her demeanour was one of a confident, in control individual, she was indeed a rare find. He shuffled over towards her, offering the tea and asking what she was looking for in his record collection.

"Oh I'm not looking for anything in particular, just seeing what you got. All the classics, a lot of stuff I've never heard of and The Beatles and Beach Boys and George Gershwin. You really are full of surprises."

"Well when you've had a life like me you get to

experience a lot of emotions and that's all music really is to me, the expression of an emotion. When you're feeling a certain way you feel inclined to listen to something that is going to enhance that mood. You know if you're going to get stoned it's better to listen to Spiritualized; it's going to work out a whole lot better than listening to some hardcore punk like Minor Threat."

"What's this?"

"Ah, indeed a rare classic of its time, a record to be only listened to under very controlled circumstances; the kings of acid fried insanity in the late 1980's, The Butthole Surfers."

"Wow, I've never heard of them but they sound great."

"Oh no, certainly not for now; it'll make you sick I promise."

"OK, hope we get to listen to it together sometime though. It sounds great."

"How about a joint; it presents a whole new way of looking at the day I promise."

"OK but not too strong ..."

"Sure, after last night, we'll just need a little jolt and we'll be fine again."

~ ~ ~

Finishing his roll-up Jack began the construction of a low-strength joint. This was another of the rituals he couldn't ditch; every day started this way; a mug of something caffeinated, roll-up or joint and then breakfast. He was pleased she seemed to like his routine.

Jack reached for a CD of George Gershwin tunes and it began to play just as he lights the joint. Rhapsody in Blue filled the room with its radiant exuberance. They moved back over to the couch were Clare sat with her legs up over Jack's thighs. He could feel himself getting stiff in his boxer shorts again.

"I can't believe it, you ready for some more already? Didn't I completely exhaust you last night?"

"I got plenty more" Jack said, passing her the joint and letting his hands begin running up and down her long and slender legs. She took a large toke on the joint and then reached over and stubbed it out in the ashtray next to the couch.

"Now what did you do that for?" he asked.

"Well, I got something else for us to do." Standing up off the couch she lifted the T-shirt off, removing it completely and then moved back towards him.

"Instead of here, how about we use the bed this time?"

"Great idea" she said grabbing his hand and moving off towards the bedroom. Disappearing under the duvet Jack couldn't quite believe his luck. She bought him to orgasm three times in the next couple of hours and by the end of it Jack was left completely fulfilled.

"Wow baby, we did great didn't we?" he said, astonished that he had both the energy and the vigour to make such a great session out of it.

"Yeah, we did real good lover," came her reply before she turned over and again feel asleep. Jack got up out of bed and moved back again towards his records. He pulled from the shelves the 1969 self-titled Velvet Underground record and within seconds Candy Says was filling his heart full of joy. It was now almost three in the afternoon and Jack had barely smoked anything so he naturally settled down in his chair, with the great music playing and finished off the joint she had put out just before their last session in bed. It tasted good, it tasted of her. Her lips had left a distinct taste to the roach-end and he luxuriated in being able to sense her even when she was asleep in the other room. He somehow didn't enjoy the next joint as much. It lacked her sweet aroma.

After the album came to a close with the rambling After Hours Jack remembered that the guys would probably be down the pub for the Sunday afternoon football. He wondered if he could persuade Clare to join him. Just as he began to think about a plan of action involving his radio being tuned in to some football show and seeing whether she expressed an opinion or not her head popped out from under the duvet.

"Hey lover, care for a wee drink this afternoon?"

"Hmm, why do I get the feeling there's some kind of hidden agenda here?"

"No reason, I just missed out on seeing my friends last night and thought, well, maybe, you'd want to meet them? I know they'll like you."

"Well when you put it like that how could I possibly say no?"

"There a weird bunch I better warn you!"

She climbed out of his bed, pulling his over-sized T-shirt on again and began moving towards the couch.

"I suppose I should get dressed shouldn't I?" she suggested.

"Can I borrow this T-shirt though? I think I could wear it as a dress if I wanted!"

"Sure thing honey, you just make sure you feel comfortable."

A few minutes later and she was ready. Even dressed like she was in nothing but her underwear and his old T-shirt she looked stunning. Pulling on her coat they set off for the pub. Jack felt the warm embrace of the last joint take hold of him and it felt like he glided to the pub. He hadn't felt this good in years.

After smoking a roll-up each to calm their nerves they arrived at the front door to the pub; the door that he hadn't been allowed through the night before, the night when everything had become very strange indeed. Holding the door open for Clare to walk through Jack saw Frank talking with a woman.

'Holy shit, Frank's with a woman too ... what is going on?' he thought to himself.

The pair had known each other from before Jack went up north to study for his Masters and Jack could never remember seeing Frank with a woman. It was just something that never happened. Whilst she wasn't as immediately as attractive as Clare it still shocked him. As the pair of them walked in Clare clutched on to Jack's arm with all her might. She was clearly nervous about the situation in to which she was walking. The football had finished and for once Jack was pleased, it meant there would be no distractions as they told stories of their respective weekends. It appeared that both Frank and him had enjoyed particularly rare weekends of joy.

"Care for a drink?" he asked as they walked towards the group.

"Sure but let me get this round. You should catch up with your friends."

"Cool, I'll have a pint but don't forget the next one is on me."

Jack moved towards his friends and reached out to shake Frank by the hand.

"Well brother, I have had one hell of a weekend, how's yours been?"

"Top notch," Frank replied without hesitation. "I met a woman, Rita, she's in the toilet at the minute and last night was a really epic night. That reminds me what happened to you?"

Jack related the story as it unfolded; the homeless group of drinkers, the alien abduction, his run-in with the new barman and then the subsequent decision to go to the new bar. At this point Clare walked over and gave Jack his pint. The sound of jaws dropping was audible over the pub's music as Jack introduced Clare to the group.

"That's where I meet this lovely creature. Clare these are the guys; Frank, Mark, Isaac and Joe. Guys, this is Clare."

"Hi," she said nervously.

With introductions out the way conversations ensued left, right and centre. It then dawned on him that he could use Frank's phone to call his own; to find out if it had too had returned from its intergalactic adventure. He found his number in the directory and called the number. It soon greeted him with a message telling him his phone was currently located in a place with no mobile signal.

'I bet,' Jack thought knowing that not even the best technology had yet been invented that could get a phone signal in outer space.

Clare felt free of any nervousness by the time she was halfway through her gin and tonic and Jack's confidence reached new levels as he finished his pint.

"Care for another?" he asked her whilst his hand gently squeezed her firm yet perfect bum through his old T-shirt.

"Sure" came her instant reply. Late afternoon slowly turned in to evening and Jack began wondering what would happen that night. Surrounded by friends and with Clare sat right next to him the idea of going to work seemed like a wild fantasy.

"Can I come back to yours again tonight?" she asked after finishing her second gin and tonic.

"Sure you can, bet it's just because my bed is so comfortable right?"

"Of course, why else would I want to come back," she said leaning in close to kiss him full on the lips. The guys looked astonished and Frank immediately made a beeline towards Rita in the hope that she would do something similar. The manoeuvre was not reciprocated and within a couple of minutes she was saying goodbye to everyone and was out the front door of the pub. Frank looked a bit dejected and Jack concluded that maybe now would be a good time for them to leave and return home.

"Well guys hopefully see you all later in the week, if not then next weekend as usual." Jack and Clare got up from their seats and after saying good-bye to the group moved towards the doorway to the pub. Clare turned to him and asked if he would mind coming back to her place instead.

"I got to get out of these clothes, get changed. Is that OK?"

"Sure, it'd be nice to see where you live ..." Jack countered before immediately worrying about his stash of weed. She lead him the right way though, towards the station. It meant walking past Jack's street so he popped in quickly and grabbed the remnants of the bottle of gin from the night before and his small bag of weed. It only took a few minutes more before they were stood outside Clare's house. She explained that she shared it with two other women who'd she known from university and who had decided to stay in London once their studies had been completed. The three of them didn't really see much of each other these days though; they had drifted apart and now only really saw each other if they happened to bump in to each other in the hall-way. She lived on the top floor and on their way up Jack followed, mesmerized by the undulations of her bum that was practically at eye level throughout the ascent. Upon reaching her door she stopped to search for her keys and Jack seized his moment. He reached under her T-shirt and pulled at her panties, removing them in one swift movement.

"What do you think you're doing mister?" she asked, teasing him by letting her tight pussy lips wrap across his probing fingers before plunging deep inside her. She squirmed and suddenly her face changed and her voice begged him.

"Oh god lover, I want you to take me here, right now!"

With instructions understood Jack pushed a couple of fingers deep inside her now damp pussy and worked his tongue in to a decent position. He licked at her now very damp pussy, plunging his tongue deep in occasionally as he felt her body quiver in pleasure. He licked enthusiastically on her clit and she began convulsing in pure wonderment of his skills with tongue and fingers. It took him about ten minutes, during which he worked himself in to a frenzy of sexual tension, to get her begging for his cock.

"I want it but not here, quick let's get to bed" she implored him, turning the key and taking his over-sized T-shirt off. He stumbled through behind her struggling to get his jeans off. It looked like a nice flat but Jack was more interested in finding the bedroom and getting what was really coming to him that night ...

SIX

The next day at work passed in a dream for Jack; all he could think about was Clare. He walked around the office that day with a really broad grin across his face, just like any middle-aged man who'd just spent a weekend of wild sex, drugs and boozing with a young beautiful woman would. It took until eleven before Jack could talk about it though. One of his colleagues, Kerry, offered him outside for a cigarette break and he seized the opportunity. Kerry was his very best friend at work, she was a special person in his life; they had grown pretty close in the six years since she had come to work in their office.

"You ain't going to be believe what I've spent all weekend doing?"

"Oh yeah, I thought something had happened to you. You seem in a very good mood today ..."

"I met a woman ... her name's Clare. She's twenty-seven and Frankly gorgeous, natural red hair, slim, curvy body, just perfect. She lives round the corner from me ..."

"Oh yes, well do tell ..."

"Oh I couldn't possibly; a gentleman always remains private on such matters. Let's just say we fucked most of the weekend, it was amazing!"

With that out of his system the rest of the morning seemed to fly by. At lunch time he went out and bought himself a new phone; nothing fancy, in fact, exactly the same one that had been taken from him to go off on its great adventure on Saturday night. The afternoon was all about watching the clock tick round to five o'clock and his moment of escape.

He had arranged to meet Clare at the train station at ten past six, the time his train usually pulled in, and they were going to her flat for some dinner and a few bottles of wine. Arriving at her flat again Jack had more time to take in what a great place she had. The living room alone was about the same size as his entire flat and looked pretty similar to his except not as over-crowded. As Clare moved off to what Jack assumed was the kitchen he began looking through he CD and DVD collections; she was clearly an old head as most people of her age just had stuff like that stored on their computer and her collection was full of classics. Jack had heard of pretty much everything on her shelves, a sure sign that she was indeed an old head on a young body.

"Do you fancy a drink lover?" she asked from what he presumed was the kitchen.

"Sure, whatever you're having make me one too. I'm easy really."

She had some pretty great rock 'n' roll in her CD collection and a fair selection of weird classics on DVD. With two gin and tonics in her hands she returned to Jack in the living room.

"You got a pretty great collection babe, impressive. Got something you fancy listening to?"

"Sure, let me put something on." She reached over and pulled The Rolling Stones album Exile on Main Street from the shelf.

"Good choice baby, now you know what I usually need

after a day at the shit-tip."

"No, but I can guess," she said, reaching for his tin on the underside of her coffee table.

"Perfect" was all Jack could say.

They snuggled up together on her sofa and her head again leant to rest on his chest. They remained this way for about half an hour, until both of them had finished their respective drinks and Clare stood up.

"Right, I'll be back in five minutes with dinner OK?"

"Sure thing, what we going to have"

"It's a surprise. You'll like it though, don't worry."

A few minutes later and she returned with two plates full of pasta and pesto. It looked delicious that's for sure.

"Here you go lover, enjoy!"

"How did you ... wow ..."

"Oh no, I didn't make it. Ruth, one of my friends, who lives on the floor below cooks for all of us. She's the only one with a cooker that works so it's her job. She don't work anyway so what else is she going to do all day, sit around and smoke and drink all day?"

"Cool, good situation you got here; lovely flat, some nice mates to share it with and even someone who'll cook for you."

A calm silence develops as they eat their food which tastes as good as it looks; it was indeed a lovely feast. Jack finished first and, getting up from the couch, asked Clare if she fancied another drink.

"Sure, but I got to have a shower after I finish dinner, hope that's OK."

"Of course babe, we all got routines!"

Bringing in two more gin and tonics Jack placed

Clare's in front of her on the topside of her coffee table. Upon completing dinner Clare took a cheeky sip of her drink, turned to Jack and kissed him and told him she'd be about twenty minutes.

Jack settled back on to her couch taking in the view. After about fifteen minutes of this he had grown bored and decided to have a better look around her flat. The room she had been in previously turned out to be a bedroom which also seemed to double-up as the bar area. The sideboards were full of random bottles and Jack moved over to examine. A good selection; a few bottles of malt whisky, a few random bottles of gin, vodka and whisky and a couple of bottles of cheap red wine.

"Hmm, an interesting collection ..." he mused to himself.

Turning towards her bed he got a heady rush from remembering some of the things they had done there the night before. It seemed most of her clothes were in a cupboard at the foot of the bed. Jack opened a random draw and was surprised to discover it full of very sexy looking underwear as well as a couple of what, at worst, could be described as interesting outfits.

"Oh what you doing lover?" he heard a voice purr behind him as he pulled out a little plaid skirt for closer examination.

"Oh nothing, just being nosey, that's all."

"You think you'd like me to dress up in that? Would it turn you on?"

"Well, maybe ..."

"It's that Britney Spears school uniform thing. When I saw that video on MTV all those years ago I knew I liked women too. She got me so hot I wondered what it would feel like to dress like that."

"That's hot lover, really hot, so you in to women as well as men? Well now that's an interesting development."

"Have you ever been with two women before in that situation?"

"Well, yeah I have, it wasn't that good babe but then I didn't fancy either of them as much as I fucking worship you."

"Oh so sweet ... now how about you go and make yourself comfortable. I'll be out in a minute or two ..."

Jack moved back in to the living room, took a swig of his drink and rolled himself a cigarette. As he light it up she appeared at the doorway, wearing that skirt, with tartan top that left very little to the imagination and a pair of white knee socks. She looked so very sexy he could feel the bulge in his boxers grow tight again. Moving over towards him she spun round and hiked her skirt up to reveal a pair of white cotton panties. Jack felt desperate to release himself from his clothing but as she approached him her arms went out and helped pull off his T-shirt and then his jeans. He sat there in just his tight boxers and salivated at the sight before him. She proceeded to put on a really sexy show for him. A slow yet explicit striptease of everything except her short little plaid skirt which she hiked up to allow him to shaft her pussy very deep as the climax. It was indeed a very long climax as Jack's mind focussed on the task at hand and giving her as much pleasure as she was giving him.

After this session Jack felt considerably more drained than previously and he knew he needed to rest. It was nearing eleven-thirty and Jack knew if he wanted to make work tomorrow he would need an early night. He grabbed her by the hand and suggested they go to bed. Once settled with her head pressed firmly in to his collarbone and her hands on his chest they soon dozed off to sleep. Jack was smiling like a kid on Christmas Day morning.

Drifting off to sleep that night he thought about the situation and it pleased him greatly. She was indeed a very special woman but it was still too early to let down his guard altogether.

SEVEN

Jack was startled awake the next morning by the sound of an alarm announcing it was seven; it had been such a relaxed night that he hadn't even noticed the alarm clock now cajoling him from his sleep. It was at least an hour earlier than he was used too and his body was unused to be so abruptly awoken. It soon became apparent that Clare was in the shower again so Jack took the opportunity to turn the alarm off and roll back over and get a few more minutes sleep. As his eyes closed slowly again he returned to the restful state pre-alarm call.

It was another ten minutes before Clare appeared; she woke him up and offered him a freshly brewed mug of coffee. It sure tasted a whole lot better than anything he could have offered her at his flat. She was dressed in a smart but still quite sexy outfit; she looked like an archetypal young businesswoman.

"What's going on? Got a job interview?"

"No, just off out to work ... didn't I tell you I run a charity shop down on the high street? It's nothing important but I got to show up today as my area manager is visiting. I got to make a good impression as I've never met him before."

"Oh I see, cool ... you look great!" Jack exclaimed taking in the whole glorious vision. The tight pinstriped skirt hugged tightly to her curvaceous bum, those gloriously long and slender legs were covered in something black whilst a tight fitting T-shirt under her suit jacket displayed an impressively pert torso.

"I'm glad you like ..." she said turning her back and lifting her skirt up to reveal a very sexy stocking and garter belt arrangement.

"If you want to give me a hand getting out of this later be here by quarter past six baby. We can have dinner and a bit of fun again tonight if you fancy?"

"I'll be here; wild horses wouldn't keep me away. I'm looking forward to it already" Jack stated matter-of-factly knowing that any hope he had of concentrating on his duties at work that day had just been blown to smithereens.

"Now where are my manners, what would you like for breakfast today?"

"Oh nothing really, I'm fine. I don't want you being late for work just to get me breakfast."

"Don't worry about that. Ruth would have been up for hours now preparing something for us all even if it's just some nice toast or cereal."

"Well in that case maybe it's time for me to meet one of your friends" Jack replied enthusiastically.

Following her down the stairs, ready to eat but also ready for work he noticed it was already nearing eight and it would soon be time for his slice of daily commuter hell. As Clare knocked on the door a woman appeared who Jack could only presume was Ruth. She was gorgeous, just as attractive as Clare, but on this occasion ever so sexier. She stood in the doorway resplendent in a tiny little nightdress. Her hair was a wild mess of dreads and the first thing that Jack smelt upon being invited in was the stench of a very strong joint, possibly one that was still burning somewhere. Ruth instructed both of them to sit on her couch.

"Now what would you like?" she asked both of them.

"Well how about some toast and a toke on that joint I can smell" Jack replied immediately.

"Well a man who comes straight to the point, now that's what I like; well done Clare!"

She busied herself preparing his toast after giving him the joint. There were maybe four tokes left; he paused after the second one and offered it to Clare.

"Not this morning lover, thanks though."

He offered it back to Ruth.

"Hey don't worry about that, plenty more where that came from."

Jack couldn't believe his luck and with his toast eaten, joint smoked, Clare and him made their way out in to the world for another day at work.

~ ~ ~

Their respective days at work dragged past, lasting what felt like an eternity, as they slowly eked towards five o'clock and escape time. Jack knew that Clare would be waiting for him in her business suit, those sexy stockings and god knows what other delights she had to offer. He could feel himself getting aroused on the train home and was practically pulling the train doors open upon finally arriving at the station. He rushed out the doors only to be left surprised by her presence on the station platform.

"Hey, thought we were meeting at yours tonight?"

"I guess I just couldn't wait that long baby, I need you now."

He wasn't sure where to go apart from either of their respective flats but as they made their way through the ticket office he felt Clare pull him off in the direction of the public toilets. She checked around the inside of the men's and then dragged Jack in after her. Within a matter of seconds he had his hard dick slamming in to her bare ass. Under the modest looking coat she had worn to meet him in was nothing but glorious naked flesh. She felt dizzy as he pummelled her sweet smooth pussy with all his desire. He just felt incredibly turned on. As they finished off and prepared to leave Jack joked that they should go back to her flat as she probably needed some clothes. Walking out the ticket hall the pair got a couple of strange looks from the team stood at the gate. Jack and Clare walked through, looking almost like a respectable business couple, knowing they had dared to open a box of tricks that would lead them to investigate a lot of their own hidden desires and predilections.

Back at the flat they talked about what had just happened whilst Ruth prepared dinner for everyone, it was indeed shaping up to be a weird evening. Ruth it appeared hadn't changed at all since this morning and had merely spent all day smoking a veritable forest of weed. Jack liked her and it appeared the feeling was reciprocated.

Dinner was great but then after Clare leads Jack back up to her flat and they settled in for a night on her couch. He was amazed at how easily they slotted in to a routine of what they perceived to be normal behaviour. It was by no means a normal life but it was slowly becoming a trusted routine that both of them could rely upon.

EIGHT

That night passed without any hint of sexual abandonment and the next morning Jack woke easily without the aid of an alarm at just after half-seven. He thought it best if this morning he went home and got changed; he'd been wearing the same clothes now for almost three days and they were starting to look really lived in. His attire at work was never called into question but occasionally his colleagues would ask him how long he'd been wearing a specific piece for; it was usually a T-shirt and Jack knew their limits were generally about three days. Therefore today would be the day he needed to change his clothes purely for the sake of his own colleagues.

With Clare awake they arranged the evening and Jack walked off home to change before going back to the station to pick up the train to work. About four stops along the line though and a couple more still from their intended destination things got very weird. The train ground to a halt and, as usual with no announcement, there appeared a bright light. It began scanning the inside of the carriage, shaking it violently. Jack had only read about what happens when UFOs started messing with trains and this had all the telltale marks of another incident unfolding right in front of his eyes. It was rare for one person to be personally involved in a number of abduction scenarios without actually being abducted but Jack knew he always had been a bit unlucky in luck. He pulled his phone from his pocket and noticed it said the time was eight forty-five. He still had a while to get to work and then suddenly the light vanished but time had very suddenly moved on to eight fifty-four. It appeared that nine minutes had gone, a time he couldn't remember, a time when anything could have happened. Jack looked around the train carriage; it was only about as half-full as it was before the bright light had come in to focus. It appeared again that the aliens had not wanted to abduct him and so somewhat fortunately he had to continue his journey to work.

The alien fleet had originally come to Earth in the mid 1950s or that is at least what Jack had learnt in History class at school. They came in peace but had wanted to examine our species; it was then that the abductions had begun. To begin with they had often taken just one, either person or animal, but recently as Jack had now witnessed twice, they had begun abducting groups of people. Jack reckoned this morning they had made off with maybe one hundred of his fellow passengers. That was just from his carriage too so maybe nearer one thousand in the whole train. He had never heard of such a large number being involved before; he knew he had been very fortunate to escape. He sat back as the train progressed to its destination thinking of what had happened to the people who'd been sat near him who had vanished during the incident. The morning had got off to a weird start, could the day get any weirder?

At work that morning a couple of his colleagues hadn't shown up. People tried calling but all they got was the same stupid message that Jack received when he had tried to call his own phone on Sunday night. The caller was in an area out of reach of any signal and it was impossible to leave a message. There was little they could do except get on with the day's work. Jack called Clare the second he heard the news on the radio about his train; he thought it best to ease her worry and to tell her that they were still on for tonight. She said simply that she would see him later at some point; it sounded like she had a plan in store for him. After such a short period of time together Jack was unsure what this would entail and the possibilities clouded his mind for the remainder of the day. What could she have in store for him that evening? Doubtless, he thought, it will be something wonderfully depraved.

NINE

Jack half-expected to see Clare waiting for him at the train station but not tonight it transpired so he headed home. It suddenly felt weird being alone; it was a feeling he had grown used to over the years but now it felt somehow odd to be sat in his living room without Clare nearby. He smoked a joint and got some dinner and still there was no sign of her. He decided to send her a text; he knew he shouldn't, it wouldn't be cool, but he felt he needed to know where she was. He really wanted to see her that much he knew.

Dinner had been a simple affair; he'd lived by himself for the best part of eighteen years and he'd learnt a few simple recipes that could be made quickly and which it was quite difficult to fuck up. His choice tonight was pasta in a green pesto sauce and despite eating it alone it tasted great; it helped that he had a bottle of wine to hand and he devoured the contents whilst whiling away the hours until her inevitable arrival. He hoped he had shown her enough in the short time they'd know each other to know that she would always return, especially on a night when they had planned to get together.

With his TV on and some random comedy on he soon grew bored; it was approaching half-eight and he still had heard no word from her. He smoked another couple of joints and suddenly it was ten and at last there was a ring at his bell.

"Hi," his voice echoed out of the battered old entry-phone system.

"It's me. I've got a surprise for you. Can I come up?"

"Sure you can ... see you in a minute."

He wasn't really sure what she had planned for him until she arrived at his front door. She was with Ruth; the pair of them had clearly been drinking and Jack seized the opportunity to join them in a tipple. Seeing as how she had shared her weed with him he also thought it fair to offer Ruth a joint that he'd built as they worked their way up the stairs to his flat.

"Well, fancy both of you turning up tonight. What's going on Clare? What's the plan?"

"I think you know," she said pulling Ruth towards her before kissing her passionately on the lips.

"Oh," was all Jack could bring himself to say. He readied himself on the couch taking in the sight of his beautiful girlfriend kissing her gorgeous friend. The kiss intensified and before long they were tugging at each other's clothes. Ruth's top was off showing off a fantastic pair of breasts clasped in a sexy black bra. Clare had removed her jeans before signalling to Jack that he should come join in. He walked behind her and kissed her on the neck, helping her out of her T-shirt at the same time. Ruth let her jeans fall to the ground and the pair of them pushed Jack back on to his couch.

"Hi," Ruth said as she moved in to kiss Jack for the first time.

"Hey," was the only word Jack could get out before her mouth was on his. His girlfriend was on her knees, pulling at his jeans and boxers, desperate to get to his cock. They eventually ended up in his bedroom and by this point they were all naked. They took it in turns to pleasure each other and Jack had never been more turned on. The night passed with the feeling that things would never be the same again. There's no turning back on this erotic odyssey from here.

The next morning he was punished for his repeated sins with an alarm call at eight and the realisation that it was still only Friday morning and him and Clare had still not known each other for a week yet. It became clear that at some point during the night Ruth had let herself out and as Jack rolled over he was pleased to see that Clare had stayed. Last night had been odd Jack thought, but at least this morning feels right.

Jack began his weekday morning routine of coffee and toast and cereal. Clare finally woke up, despite the alarm being loud enough to wake the dead, just as Jack was ready to get to work.

"Lover, where are you going?"

"I got to get to work, sorry babe, can I see you tonight?"

"Sure you can, I got another surprise for you tonight!"

Jack's mind rewound to her saying the same thing the night before and how that had ended up. He knew his mind would be thinking of all the possibilities at work that day but fortunately the day flew by and by quarter past six he was back at his home station. He had made excuses for Friday night drinks especially so he could get back to Clare. She was, he happily noticed upon disembarking, waiting for him at the station. She ran over and kissed him.

"Our six day anniversary!" she proclaimed, excitedly.

"Ah how sweet, now what you got in mind to celebrate?" came his laconic reply.

"Well, seeing as we got quite a lot out of our systems this week how about a little trip. It always feels nice travelling somewhere with a new lover; a dirty weekend maybe?"

.

TEN

It had been some time since Jack had been on a dirty weekend, he vaguely remembered a weekend in Edinburgh with an old ex that had got pretty wild but that was back in the last century. It had indeed been a long time but Jack was obviously amenable to the suggestion. After all they had done together that week it made his mind boggle as to what misadventures she would unleash on him this weekend. They decided to go to Jack's flat to kick back for a bit and have a smoke and discuss plans.

Settling in to his couch they spent little time mulling it over; Clare in fact, almost at the exact moment they sat down, announced that she wanted to go to Brighton.

"It'll be great, we can go and sit on the beach. Really relax and what's more we can stay with my friend Lisa, she's got a cool little flat down there."

"Well, it sounds like you got it all planned out. When do you think we should leave; tonight or tomorrow morning?"

"I could think of some other things to do tonight and then we could go down tomorrow, arrive about lunchtime just in time for a nice pub lunch. Sound good?"

"Sounds perfect sweet, sounds just right. How about I get us a bite to eat before we really kick back?"

"Great, just great Jack; what you going to make for us?"

"Something simple and quick I think ... pasta maybe?"

"That'll be excellent, you need any help?"

"No, no you just sit here and get stuck in to this." He reappeared from the studio room carrying a bottle of wine he'd had stashed away for a while. Two glasses and a corkscrew were in his other hand. Dinner was again a simple affair, he enjoyed cooking but not when there were such distractions as Clare in the area.

"You know what Jack? That was real nice dinner. You are a decent cook! That makes four major points for so far. You enjoy drinking and smoking, you can keep up with all my fucking and now I find out you can cook. I think my old Mum would have called you a sticker; a person you can spend a long time with."

"Cheers sweetness," was all he could respond. He had never been very good at taking compliments, especially when it amounted to so much. That night they slept in his bed and that was all they did; it was a nice chance to take a break from the constant sexual frenzy that Clare sent Jack spiralling into.

The next morning Jack woke and realised it was a Saturday. A day of routine was to be broken today but he could still start the day how he spent every other Saturday with a joint, a coffee and some toast. He began by boil the water for his coffee ensuring there was enough for the pair of them as the bread toasted. A couple of minutes passed and it was ready and Jack was back in his living room, taking up his place on his couch. The coffee worked its magic and the toast filled the small hole in his stomach before he got to attack his senses with a joint of monumental proportions. He knew he wouldn't get many opportunities to smoke so he thought he better seize the moment and spark a big one. It was a really strong one and the next thing he was aware of was Clare stood in the doorway in the T-shirt she had worn on their first visit to meet his friends in the pub.

"How you doing this morning?" she asked.

"I was doing well but now I'm doing even better" he said taking in the view of her stretching body. She looked fantastic and he knew she had woken up feeling naughty; she always seemed too and he had no complaints.

She moved over to him, leaning forward and gently kissing him on his lips. She sat down on his lap with her legs straddling his pelvis and kissed him even more passionately. He could feel himself growing excited again and he knew it was still going to be sometime before they headed off to the station and Brighton.

It was indeed a few hours later when they finally got to the station; they spent the late morning and lunchtime fucking furiously on his bed.

Jack hadn't been to Brighton for a long time but he did remember it fondly; it was a weird little bohemian town full of interesting types. The train seemed to hurtle through the countryside and within an hour they had arrived in Brighton. It seemed like half of London had decided to come and visit the town that day; the station was packed full of people but Clare still spotted Lisa waiting for them on the concourse. The pair of women ran towards each other and Jack followed at a discreet distance. Lisa looked pretty hot from where Jack stood, taking in the view. She was dressed in a tight pair of black jeans, white baseball shoes and a cool little T-shirt/ jumper combo that was red and black. She seemed to be cool and Jack felt himself getting comfortable with the situation.

"Well Jack, this is Lisa" Clare said turning her attention towards him, "she's my best mate in the whole world."

Jack, put on his more gentlemanly demeanour, extended his hand and she took it and shook. The pair expressed their commonality and conviviality in the handshake.

Lisa, now feeling completely at ease with the situation, suggested that they go and get some dinner. She explained that she only lived round the corner and they could be eating in less than half an hour.

Jack eyed Lisa up and said that it would be great to eat; it was something they had forgotten to do that morning. Their minds were on other matters and food was not on the agenda.

Clare and Jack looked at each other and began to chuckle at what they had got up to earlier. Leaving the station they turned up the hill and within a couple of minutes were at the flat. Jack was immediately jealous of the sight of the sea on the horizon and the flat seemed to be in a really nice part of town.

Lisa moved into the kitchen to prepare dinner for them all and Jack had a nose around whilst Clare vanished off to the toilet. A few minutes later and Lisa entered the living room.

"Great place you've got here seems like a nice area and all. Much better than where Clare and me live."

"Yeah I love it here; I just wish I could afford it. I'm a struggling artist and there ain't much demand for my services down here. Some months it hard to make the rent but somehow I always manage it, or at least I have so far. Unbeknown to Jack, Clare made her way in to the living room.

"So what's for dinner?" she asked, startling Jack in to realising she was stood right behind him.

"Well I just put some rice on and fancy rustling up a nice little curry. How does that sound to you two?"

"Sounds great," Jack stated, just happy to be eating anything.

After dinner the three of them sat in the living room talking and smoking. It was getting late when Jack realised he really fancied a drink.

"How about we go out for a drink? If you're a bit short of money no problem I can get the drinks in tonight," Jack announced.

"Sounds great, that's one thing about this town, there are loads of really good pubs and what's more over a hundred of them are within a twenty minute walk of my front door" Lisa extolled joyfully.

"Well what are we hanging around here for? Let's get going. Somewhere decent but that is pretty quiet. I don't want a full-on night, not after the week I've had!"

"What do you mean by that?" Clare retorted.

"Well just that it's been pretty draining and I need a rest; you've warn me out babe."

"Well, we shall see about that once we get back from the pub. I got plenty more ideas we can work on and trust me you ain't seen anything yet big boy!"

For a couple of hours they toured the bars of the North Laine and Jack couldn't quite believe how great they all were; they all seemed to have their own personality and Jack liked the feeling he got in every bar they visited.

ELEVEN

With Jack's wallet empty they left the final bar on their tour and headed back to Lisa's flat. It had been a nice evening; a chance to check out some new places and a chance to catch up with old friends in Clare's case. Jack felt comfortable in their company and the drinks went down easily and quickly.

At the flat about twenty minutes later Jack collapsed in to a space on Lisa's couch and proceeded to roll a really strong joint. Clare vanished off somewhere whilst Lisa made herself comfortable opposite Jack after sorting out some music for them all to listen too.

The sounds of sixties Motown filled the living room with their cool moves; it was Martha Reeves and The Vandellas.

"Did I ever tell you my Martha Reeves story?" Jack asked Lisa.

"No but I bet it's a great story ..."

"A couple of years ago I meet her at a festival, she was a really cool lady. I phoned my Dad and handed the phone to Martha. She said hi Jack's Dad, I hear you're a big fan of mine to him before handing the phone back to me. He didn't believe it was her and even after I showed him pictures of me and her taken on that day I still don't think he believes it was her."

"Really that's a really great, funny story! Why didn't your Dad believe it was her?"

"No idea ..."

The conversation came to an abrupt halt as Clare appeared in the doorway to the living room. She was dressed in a dressing gown having, Jack guessed, just taken a shower. She radiated a real wonderful sexiness and Jack looked over at Lisa unsure of how she would react.

"Come here big boy," was her simple instruction to Jack and he complied. She took his T-shirt and jeans off and he stood there in the middle of the living room feeling his balls tighten and his cock stiffen. Lisa walked over to Clare and the pair began kissing. Jack moved back to the couch and relaxed, taking in the show that was unveiling before him. The three of them were soon writhing around on the floor in all kinds of positions, desperate to get off. By the time they had finished it was late, very late indeed and Jack needed to get to bed. He was completely exhausted and drained.

~ ~ ~

The next day came into view over a couple of naked female bodies that were sharing the bed with him. He was unsure of the time but assumed it was probably nearing lunchtime and it was time for him to get back on routine. It was Sunday after all and therefore it was time for a coffee and a joint. He would wait until Lisa and Clare woke up before more substantial food could be thought of. As the joint began to take grip on his mind he began remembering some of the scenes from last night. It had been a truly amazing experience.

By the time Clare finally appeared Jack was zonked out on the sofa having smoked himself in to a stupor quickly. She looked at him and smiled. She would help wake him up by brewing some fresh coffee. The water boiled quickly and soon Lisa had joined Jack in the living room. The pair of them looked exhausted but happy until Clare walked out carrying coffee; their blessed relief. The coffee energised the trio in to conversation and it wasn't long before Clare dropped a bombshell that Jack had not seen coming.

"I was just thinking of moving down here with her; you know she's been having trouble making rent and I thought with my help ... well ..."

"What? Are you saying what I think you're inferring?"

"No, not if you think we are splitting up. No way, I was hoping you'd move down here with us. You saw yesterday how easy it was to get here so how about it?"

Jack couldn't quite believe what he was hearing and had no idea of how to respond; it sure would take some thinking over before he could reach such a huge decision.

The afternoon passed with him deep in thought, could he commute to his job in London, could he afford it, what would happen to his old friends back at home? There were a million questions racing through his mind but it was clear from the second that they sat down to dinner that Clare's propaganda programme had begun.

"Tell Jack how fantastic it is down here in Brighton Lisa ..."

"Brighton is a great town, only an hour to London and I can promise freshly cooked meals for you every night when you get in from work. Add in all the cool little shops and bars and the huge amount of weed grown down here, I can't see what you've got to think about."

"Plus, of course," Clare continued, "you get the chance

to bed two beautiful sexy women whenever you want to."

"Well, I've got to say it sounds like a great plan but I've got to think about it and work out money. If I can though you know the answer will almost certainly be a resounding yes."

"Great, now is there anything we can do to persuade you any further."

Jack merely grinned and the conversation continued. They talked music, books, art, everything that Jack loved talking about. Jack felt like he was in heaven; it was a beautiful feeling and that night he got to fuck the pair of them again. Lisa really was a wild woman; she never seemed to get enough. Even that night, after all they had done over the course of the last thirty-six hours, she seemed desperate for more sexual activity. The three of them settled down on to her bed and the frenzy returned; Jack was all over both of them, fucking Clare in her pussy, Clare fucking Lisa with a strap-on in her pussy as Jack fucked her other holes. It was a wild night and as Jack finally began to drift off to sleep the first rays of sun began appearing over the nearby South Downs. He knew he would never get to work that day; he didn't care particularly and it felt good for him to fuck-up.

When he finally woke later, he soon realised it was much later, he checked his phone. There had been no missed calls; why hadn't any one phoned from work. It was odd that no one had called to check up on him, to find out where he was rather than where he should have been. He decided to call and see what was going on. There was no answer and most bizarrely of all when the answer-phone kicked in it was with the message he had heard his old phone tell him when it was in the clutches of its intergalactic adventures.

TWELVE

When Jack finally got back to London he was alone again and for the first time since he had met Clare he was glad to get some space; he had a lot to think about. He had never particularly liked living where he currently was; it was only meant to be a stopgap after university but it had been a full decade and the area had got a lot worse than when he had moved in originally. He had been looking for a way out, a means to escape, for a long, long time now but could this really be it? Was the idea of moving to Brighton with a woman he barely knew a real solution; all relationships end at some point so what would happen once the inevitable happened? It was a hard choice but every time he thought about Clare, that body, that brain, everything, he knew he had to go with her. She was unlike any women he had ever met and maybe, just maybe this was the opportunity he had been waiting for.

The streets outside his house were not safe, whether it be the alien menace, the derelict street-drinkers or the army of muggers who stalked them. Despite having very little he was still the target of muggers and he'd been robbed on a number of occasions; he felt it was only a matter of time before something very bad happened.

The house was a dilapidated wreck and Jack was the only long-term tenant; the kids who invariably shared the house with him came and went with what appeared alarming regularity, usually after only six months, the minimum length of tenancy. He was eyed with suspicion by all the newcomers as if there was something criminal about a man of his age only having the money to live in a house which they had all assumed would only be fit for poor kids. It was expected that by his stage in life he should at least have a career, a family or at least enough money to escape. He had none of that and with life as it currently was this was a situation unlikely to change unless he went with Clare to Brighton.

There was, as is so often the case in Jack's life, the subject of money; could he afford to move to Brighton and once there could he afford to live. The train fare would be astronomical but hopefully the rent, especially split three ways, would hopefully be lower. He hated crunching numbers but after a lifetime of living just above the poverty line it was something he had become adept at doing. A couple of hours later and his research had been done; it did appear that he could, just about, afford it. Now all he had to think about was his heart. Could his heart handle a relationship with such a red-blooded woman? His heart had been hurt many times before but at least then he had a group of friends to fall back on; in Brighton he would effectively be alone without Clare and who knew by the time it ended who was to say he could even afford a move back to London? It was a situation that needed a lot more consideration; Jack decided to give it another week before making a final decision, he would talk to all the key players and give serious thought to all that they said. He needed to approach the situation as an adult and not a yearning lustful youth; at thirty-nine years old it was about time he started acting like an adult.

THIRTEEN

Jack woke up the next morning in his own bed, alone for once and seemingly well rested. The first thought that entered his head was of Clare and where she had spent the night; it seemed inevitable that she was still in Brighton at Lisa's flat. He wondered what they had got up to on the night he missed. If it involved Clare he reasoned that it had to have featured some form of perversion. He rolled over in bed and rubbed his cock through his boxer shorts.

"Shit, a hard-on like this and no one to share it with!" he muttered finally climbing out of bed. At last he looked at his phone and noticed it was still only eight so he could at least go in to work. It would be good for his mind to have other things to think about. Turning to his TV he selected one of the News channels and on the screen was a picture of where he worked.

"Historic house ... centre of London ..."

"Oh shit, what's going on?" Jack thought as he watched the coverage unfold on the TV screen in front of him. He sat on his couch and watched the coverage continue. It appeared that on Sunday night the building had been trapped in some form of alien force-field; that would explain the odd message his phone call had elicited the previous morning at least. Since then, all the artwork had been taken and those who were in the building at the time, a number of security guards mainly, had been abducted. Eventually they announced that the building

Dive

had been freed from the alien menace and that hopefully
the situation would return to normal later that morning.
Jack threw on some clothes and walked out the front door;
it was going to be, for once, an interesting day at work.

Walking down The Strand towards work it was
noticeable how easy it was to get around. The pavements
were, in comparison to a normal day, relatively empty;
Jack's eyes looked up to the sky. Above him was a huge
UFO, so huge in fact that the edge of it disappeared in to
the horizon. It was a strange sight but Jack knew there was
nothing he could do about it. He had got lucky yesterday
with work; he could just tell them he heard the news and
had decided to try and call in. If he didn't go in today he
would be in trouble and that was something he couldn't
afford. Not now, not with his life in such an interesting yet
perilous position.

Entering the Institute he was pleased to see Stacey, the
young receptionist, sat behind the desk.

"Morning Stacey, how's it going?" he asked on his way
through.

"It's getting pretty weird isn't it? Think we'll be alright
today though don't you Jack?"

"Let's damn well hope so. I don't want to be abducted
and experimented on by a bunch of weird little grey
creatures that's for sure!"

She laughed but it was a nervous laugh knowing that
at any moment Jack's worst-case scenario could become a
real situation. Jack continued up the stairs to the office. By
nine-thirty all his colleagues had turned up with the
exception of one; his big boss, her train had been involved
in an incident as she was on the phone to her PA Susan

that morning. She had relayed the news of what had happened as the news coverage on her computer was actually at the scene. They reported the now familiar scenario of a train being intercepted and the mass abduction of most of the passengers; to the news reporter it seemed like a normal every day kind of incident. They were becoming so frequent now that they barely got more than a couple of minutes coverage in any news broadcast.

Work passed pretty quickly that day and Jack at least got to talk to Kerry about Clare's proposal over a nice relaxed lunch. She agreed it was a sensational opportunity and as regards his relationships with people in London, well that wouldn't change. Why should it? He would still work at the Institute and he'd still be around for five days a week. She argued that nothing would really change except the journey and where he lived. Jack spent most of the afternoon getting up to date with the filing whilst thinking about all that Kerry had said. It had been a very persuadable argument.

~ ~ ~

That night he went back home for what could potentially be one of the last times and as he got to the station he was pleased to see Clare waiting for him just outside the ticket office. They ran in to each other's arms and kissed passionately as if they had been separated for years and not just a day.

"Hey lover, how's your day been?"

"Good thanks, work was OK and I had a good chat with a friend about your offer."

"Oh yeah, what did they say?"

"She reckons I'd be crazy to not go with you; so that's one in your favour."

71

They went back to Jack's flat and ate a simple dinner and drank a decent bottle of red wine. The evening was developing nicely and for once everything seemed to be quite normal as Jack settled back in to his couch. That, however, was all to change as Clare returned to the living room from the toilet. With a wry grin developing across her face she turned to him and asked, quite simply, "Do you know what I want us to do tonight lover?"

He looked at her, unsure what she had in mind. The previous week had already blown his mind as well as many loads of his bodily fluids and it showed no sign of slowing down now with whatever she had in her mind. She was unlike any other women he had met and it seemed no matter how depraved her mind could get he was always keen to participate. She pulled her coat apart to show off that sexy Britney outfit she'd wowed him with on one of their first nights at her flat. With her coat open her hands lifted her skirt to reveal those damn sexy white cotton panties.

"Oh you are feeling very naughty tonight aren't you my sexy minx?"

He stood up and began walking towards her but she stood up straight and lowered the skirt to cover her panties.

"Not here, not now. I want you to fuck me in the park, I want it to look like your fucking a young girl in the park you dirty old man, you sleazy bastard."

"Really... shit, that sounds both really amazing but also quite dangerous. What happens if we get caught? Some fairly unlikable types hang around up there. Perverts, street drinkers and drug dealers, you know the type."

"Of course I do, I feel like one of them."

"Well so do I sometimes but it's not something I'd

particularly like to advertise. I love fucking outdoors, you know that, but with you wearing that? I could get killed if the wrong kind of person catches us."

"It'll be fine I promise, just keep remembering I'm twenty-seven years old, I'm not a real school girl, you are a pervert but not a really evil one. It's just a bit of harmless fun."

"Well when you put it like that and the thought does turn me on incredibly, how could I say no?"

"We got to go right now though otherwise I'm just going to have to fuck you here... you know that outfit always gets me feeling naughty. Are you going to wear your hair in pigtails? "

"If you would like me to, I'll do anything for you."

She tied her coat back up, covering everything from her neck down to just below her knee, before allowing his hand to grab hers to lead her out the front door of her flat. By the time they had got to the front door of the house Jack was already close to exploding. He could feel his cock stiffen inside his boxers and knew it wouldn't be long before he got that blessed release that his body so craved. Exiting she turned to smile at him; she had never looked happier, it seemed the more dangerous the situation the more she got off on it. He was beginning to wonder how it would ever come to an end, especially now with the pair of them on the way to the park with her wearing a school girl outfit and ready to let him fuck her in the bushes. As they got to the park they ran towards the darkest area and in to the bushes. She took her coat off and lay down on the ground maneuvering her leg so that her skirt rode up, exposing a flash of white panties. Her blouse was held together by only one button, it soon popped free to reveal a bra-less chest. She looked spectacular. Jack decided at first to begin with her panties and getting her as hot as he currently was. He lowered his tongue down and flicked at her pussy through her panties. It tasted good, it tasted quite damp already. Pulling her panties down he buried his tongue deep inside her whilst allowing his hands to wander up to play with her breasts. As he rubbed over her nipples he felt her hand grab his. It was clear she was enjoying herself as the first little moan was elicited from her mouth.

"I want you inside me lover, get your cock deep inside me." Jack didn't hesitate pulling his jeans and boxers down ready to lunge his stiff cock deep into her now wet pussy. She was clearly turned on and it wouldn't be long before both of them would reach fulfillment. They both collapsed in a heap almost as soon as they had vanquished their desire. Turning to kiss him on the cheek a broad grin appeared across her face.

"That was amazing lover, god you really know what to do!" she purred doing her blouse back up as well as pulling her panties, left in the heat of passion just around her ankles, back up. Jack pulled his jeans and boxers back up and smiled the smile of a man who'd just fulfilled a long-held fantasy.

Walking back through the park she turned to him and grabbed his hand.

"Am I your Queen? Do you think of no one but me? I know you do and as such I know you are going to move with me down to Brighton. It's something we need to do; it just felt so right down there didn't it and I know you fancy Lisa and I know you'll be cool with us sharing her occasionally. How does that sound you dirty old man?"

"It's true, you are my Queen! I will follow you to the ends of the world just to be with you."

That was that then, it appeared a decision had been made and Jack and Clare would be moving to Brighton. As soon as they got home Clare pulled out her phone and texted Lisa with the news; a two-bed flat/house would be needed, a maximum of a thousand a month rent.

As night fell Jack's mind couldn't stop thinking about the move, the implications of the move he had seemingly just agreed to undertake. At least he reasoned it wouldn't happen immediately, it was inevitable that it would take some time to get everything into place and besides when it was time to move he didn't own much apart from his books, records and films. He began wondering who could help with the big move, as far as he was aware none of his friends could drive. Jack had never bothered to take any driving lessons as having grown up in London with the idea that he would never leave he thought it pointless. It was only now that his parents had gone and he needed a driver that he regretted not taking the chance to learn. He hoped that Clare had thought about the problem and would already have a solution lined up; in fact he was sure that Clare would sort every last detail out for them. She was the one who seemed more desperate for a new life in a new town. He thought she was increasingly become the one, the one he wanted to spend forever with.

FOURTEEN

The rest of the week passed without much incident; Jack and Clare continued to go to work and their evenings were spent curled up on the settee in Jack's flat. They would drink wine, watch movies, listen to music and smoke weed; Jack had introduced his routine to Clare and she had taken to it with joy. Her joy gave the whole routine a freshness that Jack had never thought was needed but now it felt fantastic to have that new dynamic in his life. A lot of their conversation was taken up with their move to Brighton and what it would be like for the both of them, what they could do down there.

On Thursday evening the dream came closer to reality with a phone-call from Lisa. She had looked at a few places but they had largely been dumps and not suitable at all, not in the right area of town or too run-down. The dream seemed a long way off but Lisa promised to keep looking. It seemed she was just as desperate for the move as Clare was growing in London.

Jack told her not to worry, things would improve and she should keep faith, something would come up soon he promised. He didn't know why he sounded so convinced by this summary but, maybe, he was finally getting used to things working out for him. That was one of the great things that had happened since he'd met Clare; his confidence had grown and life in general just seemed a whole lot better.

The weekend came and went with Clare and Jack barely leaving the bedroom; they were both voracious for more sexual delinquency and that was all that mattered for either of them. Clare had dressed up in some sexy outfits whilst they had played out some roles in their own homemade porn films; it was a wild time of no rules, a time where the limits were stretched to breaking point. Jack had filmed himself fucking Clare in her Britney outfit; she was playing up the innocence and naivety of the little schoolgirl getting fucked for the first time. It seemed the role that Clare had really taken to however was that of the dominatrix, a role she took very seriously. For the first time she tied Jack up and teased him to the point where he was begging to released so he could fuck her. It was that kind of weekend.

~ ~ ~

The following week was ticking over very nicely until Thursday evening when Lisa called. She wanted to talk to Clare this time; she had news but she wanted to tell her rather than Jack first.

"I've found somewhere, it's amazing!" Jack heard Lisa announce loudly to Clare. Jack got Clare to put the call on speaker, he couldn't quite believe how excited he'd suddenly become.

"It has a high ceiling and is almost like a warehouse space but it's on one of those lovely squares that overlook the sea. It even has a third bedroom that the previous tenants used as a studio for their art. It's amazing!"

"Wow," Clare muttered, quite dumbstruck.

"So what's the plan?" Jack chipped in.

"Well can you get down here to view it? I've made an

appointment for Saturday. I hope that's alright Jack, I thought if it was then you could come down and check it out too."

The next day flew by and almost in an instant it was Saturday morning and Jack and Clare were sat on the train heading south out of London for a weekend in, what could be by the end of the day, a place that was soon to be home. Brighton was two stops away and forty minutes but it felt like a lifetime away.

The glorious late autumn morning that was unfurling outside just added to the pair's anticipation. The masses of sweating humanity that shared their carriage escaping London also felt a heightened anticipation of fun. For some it was for the day, others for the weekend, for a pair of them possibly a new life.

FIFTEEN

"I better call Lisa, check everything is alright for today," Clare announced pulling her phone from her bag that sat on her lap.

"Hey, it's me. How's it going today? Are you ready for our imminent arrival?"

"We've just gone through Horley, should be about fifteen minutes I reckon. Are you waiting for us?"

"Cool, well better go. See you soon."

"She's waiting for us at the train station."

"Cool, so what's the plan?"

"Well, the flat viewing is at 2pm. Shall we go dump our stuff at Lisa's and go and get a pub lunch or something near the viewing. You know, check out the local options."

"Sounds good, maybe we could just make it coffee and sandwich though; flat viewings are one vital thing you always need to be sober and clear-headed for. I've ended up living in some real holes just as a result of turning up stoned for the flat viewing. We are already excited enough I think that we must keep a clear head. If this place is half as good as Lisa reckons..."

"Sounds like a plan," Clare responded before tucking her arm into his and gazing out the window at the countryside that was passing by outside the train. It was a beautiful sight.

"Can you imagine being a commuter on this line; it must almost be a pleasure to travel."

"Ah well, don't get too carried away, that's one of the first things I need to get sorted if we move. I can't do this every day, it'd be too expensive and I'd be out for almost ten hours a day."

"I see your point; maybe any route to work is a bad one because it's going to work."

"I don't want what happened to Diana to happen to me either, you remember I told you about my boss's abduction didn't I?"

"Yeah, bit scary..."

"And you know something those homeless types who stole my phone still haven't returned."

Clare started chuckling to herself.

"You could be the only human being who wants to be abducted Jack!"

They both laughed before falling silent as the train started to travel through the northern Brighton suburbs. The anticipation all around rose to a new high as the train pulled in a little after eleven.

Approaching the ticket barrier the pair saw Lisa standing there waiting for them.

"Wow Jack, look at Lisa. Doesn't she look fine and sexy?"

"Hmm, she does" Jack agreed taking in the view of Lisa. Her tight little denim skirt hugged to her now impressive looking bum, a plain black T-shirt with pale green V-neck jumper pulled over the top. To top it all off was a pair of green and black stripy tights. That was the clincher; Jack had always had a thing for women in sexy underwear and stripy tights.

"I love her stripy tights babe," Jack whispered in

Clare's ear as they walked through the ticket barrier.

Lisa came running over.

"Hi!" she exclaimed, excited at seeing her friends return with the possibility that they would soon be here full-time. She hoped they liked the flat as much as she did; her life in Brighton was a lonely existence. She had a few friends but never enough money to go out and socialize to widen that circle.

The pair walked over and both went to kiss Lisa, Clare got there first but Jack was more than willing to wait. He moved in, swept Lisa back and kissed her passionately across her lips. Clare did nothing but smile whilst Lisa swooned in Jack's arms.

"Well shall we go dump all your stuff at mine and then venture out for some lunch?" Lisa suggested as if reading her guests minds'.

"Sure," came the response from the pair at the same time.

~ ~ ~

Back at the flat Clare got changed in to some of Lisa's clothes; she'd been wearing the same clothes now for the best part of three days and she was starting to smell a bit, not that Jack minded in the least.

Fresh from the shower Clare looked stunning in a short tight black dress and her leather coat. Her legs were clad in black nylon whilst her feet wore a pair of boots.

"Wow babe, you look amazing!" Jack enthused as she entered the room and his frame of vision.

"Ah thanks sweets, glad you like,"

"Oh yes, amazing how well an old scrubber like you can spruce herself up with the right choice of clothes isn't it?" Lisa deadpanned.

"Oh you bitch," Clare drawled, holding back the desire to laugh, "… now shall we go get some lunch?"

~ ~ ~

Walking back past the train station and in to the center of town Jack was astonished at the amount of people that were around. He asked Lisa if this was common.

"Oh yeah, all those damn out-of-towners and visitors from London mean we're rammed every weekend of the year. It can get a bit tiresome but for the other five days its bliss."

"Glad to hear it, most of these people remind me of why I want to escape London!"

Lisa decided to take them straight to the house and then find a café from there.

"It makes sense, since Wednesday there could be a new café nearby that is really good. Chances are there ain't but I know a real good one nearby anyway," Lisa explained as the trio walked down an alleyway and suddenly before them appeared a huge Georgian square. It was vast with a green area in the middle, lying on the grass was a couple, quaffing wine and eating a picnic. It was an atypical English scene and when Lisa announced that this square was where the flat was located Jack's anticipation for the viewing became almost uncontrollable.

"Really?" was all he could muster as Lisa told Clare and him it was at number twenty-three, on the top floor of the building. Jack stopped and took in the scene; it was beautiful and a vast improvement on the area where Clare and him lived in London.

"There's a nice little café on the corner too with

outside seating so we can smoke if you want to?"

"Well sure I do, now I know what we've got in store for the afternoon I could do with a smoke just to calm myself down."

"Wow, Jack, are you excited?" Clare asked.

Sitting outside the café the three ordered coffee and an ashtray and Jack began chain-smoking whilst sipping his drink. Silence feel as the three contemplated where their respective lives could be in less than an hour from now. Things could change forever in that short period of time.

SIXTEEN

As the group left the café they were all excited but desperately trying to hold together the image of being completely in control. They wanted to present the image of people who looked at places like they were just about too on a regular basis, as if they'd always lived in such, hopefully, palatial surroundings.

"Well, what do you think?" Lisa asked as they arrived outside number twenty-three.

"It looks amazing," Jack said before retreating a little, "... is all of the top floor ours?"

"That's what it looked like on Wednesday," Clare confirmed.

"Hmmm," Jack meditated, "... could be okay," he pondered, feeling a nervous excitement run through his body.

"Only nine-hundred a month though, at three-hundred each it's cheaper than anything else I've seen and by a long distance the very best one."

"Well let's just wait and see," Clare confirmed, ending the conversation.

A young rather straight looking man approached them wearing a suit and Lisa walked over to greet him.

"So," he began, "this must be Jack and Clare?"

"Yeah," Jack said in his manliest of tones, "I'm Clare..."

All four of them started to laugh and any nervousness

was dispelled with that smart quip. The young man introduced himself as Adam.

"Well, shall we go take a look?" Adam asked as the key turned in the front door.

The entry-hall was grand; a broad sweeping staircase dominated with a flat to the side. Jack followed the group up the stairs, transfixed by the undulations of Clare's bum through Lisa's tight black dress. He wanted to grab it, get her attention and kiss her for what they were all about to receive. Arriving outside a door that seemed to be the only entrance to the top floor Adam turned and announced that this was it.

As the group walked in Jack's jaw dropped whilst Clare began to physically shake. Lisa and Adam walked in and Adam immediately went on the hard sell. There was nothing to sell though as Jack and Clare were already picturing themselves living there. The main living room had a kitchen at the back with a huge amount of space between there and the floor-to-ceiling sash windows that presented an amazing view of the pier that had burnt down and the sea that dominated towards the horizon.

"So this is the main living space but I guess you'll want to see the bedrooms," Adam continued leading them off to the left of the door and down a corridor.

"Here is the first, the biggest ..." he intoned opening the door. Clare and Jack feel through the door and Jack stood aghast at what he saw. With Adam turning and heading out towards the other bedroom Jack turned and whispered in Clare's ear, "This room is bigger than my whole flat!"

The second bedroom was almost as big and Lisa

smiled as if silently acknowledging that this was to be her room.

"Here is the third bedroom. The last tenants used it as a studio, you can do with it whatever you like but I understand that Lisa is an artist so..."

"Another room, wow, this is something else," Jack finally said, dropping all pretense at the idea of being a hard sell.

"Now, let's talk money," Jack announced taking Adam under his arm and leading him back towards the living room.

"Are any bills included in this nine-hundred a month?"

"Yes, because you share a bathroom with downstairs all council tax and water rates are included in the rent. The electric is on a meter, it works out quite cheap by all accounts, and that's it. There's a phone-jack in the corner of the kitchen and a TV signal connector by the windows down there. Is there anything else?"

"Well," Jack said, bracing himself for the announcement, "... where do we sign?"

Clare and Lisa started cheering in delight, jumping up and down like over-excited kids on Christmas morning.

Adam pulled a document out of his bag and handed it to Jack to peruse. He read it thoroughly as they walked back into the main room and down the stairs to the main entry hall to the block. Reaching the bottom stair Jack turned to him and asked, "So you got a pen?"

Adam handed over the pen and Jack signed before passing it to Clare and Lisa as well.

"We can move in a month but I hope you understand

it can't be any sooner as I've got a lot of loose-ends to tie up in London. I've a whole past life to pack-up in less than a month..."

Jack could feel a cold chill develop down his back and suddenly he was struck with an inexplicable fear; was he going to enter a situation that was simply way-in over his head? It would be an interesting time that was for sure.

SEVENTEEN

It felt like the longest month ever as Jack waded through a whole host of bureaucratic bullshit from the council, trying to find a man with a van big enough to take all their stuff in one trip and most worryingly of all, his own growing emotion at the major transformation that was just about to take his life off down a new path, changing it forever. He would often find himself lying awake at nights either worrying or being excited about the imminent change.

Bizarrely during this whole episode his phone had returned; Jack simply woke up one morning and it was on his bedside table. He knew it would be unwise to try and work out what exactly had happened to it or how it had been returned to his possession so he didn't think about it too deeply. The amount of alien activity had increased during the week it was returned but Jack had still not seen any of the group of men who'd stolen his phone in the first place. He supposed that they could have been returned someplace else but again that was something he didn't particular want to think about, he already had a whole host of things to think and worry or grow excited by.

The alien activity was as natural a part of the world to Jack as a tree or a human even though he had never actually seen an actual entity just the crafts in which they would travel. There was a lot of talk amongst Jack's friends that they were indeed secret military planes, designed to look like generic UFOs, carrying out orders from some secret government. Jack could see the reasoning behind this as no major seats of government had yet been attacked and with the masses living in fear of being abducted at any time those in power largely got away with whatever they wanted. It was a scary time for humanity but it seemed those at the top had still yet to come to grips with what was going on. The attack on Jack's workplace had only clarified that it seemed anyone outside of a tiny elite should be worried. If, he thought, working for a world-renowned art institute full of rich and powerful people's kids would mean he was safe-guarded against any kind of alien threat he was proved wrong the second they seized that first Cezanne.

~ ~ ~

Eventually the morning arrived, the morning of the big move. It was a Saturday towards the end of what had been a glorious late summer and a battered old Transit van pulled up outside Jack's place. He had already been awake for a few hours and had begun taking his stuff down to the entry hall. The man with the van charged by the hour and Jack knew it would take a while to load up his gear. His furniture, what little of it there was, went in first; a two-seater sofa, an armchair and a couple of cabinets chock full of paper. Then it was the turn of his rather ancient pieces of technology, his old TV, a decrepit old stereo system and his rather plush but in fact second-hand laptop before finally his records, books, films and clothes. When it had all been loaded the van was about three-quarters full and Jack was grateful that Clare didn't own that much stuff in comparison to all his junk. It had taken almost an hour to load up his belongings but when they turned up at Clare's she simply stood on the pavement with a large suitcase full of clothes, a small box of records and books and not much else. The van headed out towards Croydon, destined for the start of the A23 that would lead them all the way through the countryside to their new town, their home for who knew how long.

It took a couple of hours for the drive, the traffic was bad due to lots of visitors pouring in to Brighton to soak up the last of the warm summer days by the beach, but when they arrived Jack was delighted to see someone waiting for them outside.

"Hi," she greeted them, " ...you look like Jack to me. I'm Paula, I work as Adam's assistant and he's sent me over today to give you the keys."

"Excellent, sorry if we're a bit later than you expected but the traffic was pretty bad."

"It's no problem, I only live around the corner and I tipped off a neighbour to let me know when they saw you arriving."

She handed Jack the keys and he passed them over to Clare who immediately ran in the entry hall of the old building, heading Jack suspected for their flat. The driver came round the back of the van and unlocked it. Jack climbed in and began the long process of moving the stuff up the three flights of stairs to the top floor. He was glad when he saw the driver follow, helping him get the boxes to the flat. With the two of them working flat-out it took less than half-an-hour to complete the job and suddenly they were done, they were home.

When Jack dumped the last of the boxes on the living-room floor he turned and offered the driver a tip for helping him bring all the stuff up which was gladly accepted. With the driver out the way Jack turned to Clare and walked towards her.

"We done it babe, we fucking done it," he said swinging her in to his arms before kissing her passionately. Within minutes they were in the main bedroom naked with Jack on top of her grinding his dick deep in to her moist damp pussy. It was only once they finished fucking that they finally began to realise that it was all real; that this was the dawning of a new period in their respective lives.

Rolling off her Jack climbed off the bed and walked in to the living room in just his boxer shorts, which he pulled on over his long legs before leaving the bedroom. He walked in to the living room and walked to a box containing some of his belongings and pulled from it his tobacco tin. It had ceased being a place for tobacco a long time ago, it was now where he kept his ubiquitous supply of pot. Grabbing it and his tobacco pouch and papers he moved towards the two-seater sofa positioned in the middle of the living room. Sitting down he immediately began the usual routine. Paper flat, tobacco spread, pot sprinkled, roach constructed and finally the flourish of the rolling, which finished with a beautiful joint ready to be smoked. He took it in between his lips and sparked it to life.

Clare came walking in to the living room wearing a pair of black panties and a tight black vest top.

"We should probably phone Lisa and tell her it's safe for her to come down now shouldn't we?"

"Yep," Jack concurred after inhaling deeply.

~ ~ ~

It was another hour or so before Lisa arrived and by this point Jack had the munchies really bad; he was on his third joint of the session when Lisa rang the buzzer to the flat and Jack had it in his mind to go for a fish and chip supper somewhere.

Clare pulled on some jeans and ran down to help Lisa up with her stuff as Jack brewed the kettle hoping that Lisa had bought some food and drink supplies with her.

Lisa walked in to the living room first carrying with her two suitcases and dressed in a knee-length black skirt with a plain red T-shirt, black leggings and a pair of old trainers.

"Hi Jack," she said as he helped her over the threshold with her stuff.

"Hey Lisa, how's it going?"

"Yeah, pretty good. She's a pretty little helper ain't she?" Lisa asked just as Clare walked through the door carrying three boxes loaded so high she couldn't see over the top of them.

"Shit Clare, let me give you a hand!" Jack asked upon realising and grabbing the top two boxes of the pile.

With the three of them finally home Jack smiled before being told that there was more stuff downstairs.

"Would you be a sweetie?" Clare asked him.

It took Jack two trips up and down the stairs before all of Lisa's stuff was finally sitting in the living room.

"Now, after all that I fancy some dinner" Jack declared.

"Sure, what do you fancy?" Lisa asked.

"Well seeing as were in Brighton how about fish and chips?"

"Swell," Lisa deadpanned.

They spent the next few minutes discussing the myriad of options for places to eat before deciding that the nearest place would suffice. It was only going to be a fish and chip supper; it surely couldn't cost that much wherever they went.

It was a few hours later and after a real feast helped down with litres of wine that Jack realised just how expensive his new town was. Three bottles and a supper each and it came to nearly sixty pounds. He was very happy when Lisa and Clare announced they should split it three ways and he pulled a new crisp twenty-pound note from his wallet and placed it on top of the bill. They soon followed suit and as they were leaving the restaurant Lisa suggested the idea of a couple more bottles back at the flat.

Despite the restaurant only being a few minutes' walk from their flat they still had two options as to where to buy their wine. Jack decided the best course of action would be another three bottles, one good one and two of the bargain bin options. Lisa pointed to a sign in the second off-licence advertising two bottles for five pounds and Jack lead the three of them in.

"I think three more red, don't you?" he asked Clare turning towards her whilst inspecting a bottle of Spanish Rioja.

"Sure, why not. We can get a nice one and it'll still only work out at ten pounds for three!" she said moving over towards the stacks of two-for-one offers and immediately picking two of the shelf marked '2 bottles for £5'. The three came together at the counter and began counting out the money.

Five minutes later and they were back at the flat and Clare was uncorking the good bottle as Jack rolled a bigger, stronger joint for all of them to consume.

By the end of the third bottle the party had died down to a quiet drunken slur. Jack struggled to his feet and announced that he was off to bed and Clare jumped up and followed him off to bed. He passed out almost instantly, only faintly aware of his girlfriends' hands delving in to his boxer shorts hoping to get some kind of reaction from his flaccid, limp dick. There was to be no joy for either of them that night as Jack drifted off, snoring as he went.

EIGHTEEN

Sunday dawned with the glorious sun pouring in through the living room windows and, through the gap between door and frame wide open, ebbing in to the bedroom where Jack lay. He was surrounded by both Clare and Lisa and as his eyes struggled to open a broad smile fixed upon his face. Suddenly feeling a deep dark throbbing that was only too familiar he knew what was happening. He could feel the waves of the impending hangover building inside his head, aware that he probably needed to be sick.

'Damn those couple of cheap bottles,' he thought whilst running off to the bathroom. He knew it was going to be a hard morning; there were a lot of jobs that needed to be done in the flat. It was going to be a long haul but Jack knew if it worked out it would be like living in a dream. He vomited in to the toilet and flushed it immediately knowing that if he saw his deposit he would feel the need to repeat until he got it all out of his system. He slowly began to feel more human and moved his attention to the sink where he ran the cold tap, scooping up handfuls of it and splashing his face and running the dampness through his long bedraggled hair. Looking in the mirror it came to him that he was quickly becoming an old man, an old man with a hot younger girlfriend but still. It was unavoidable; Jack's fortieth birthday was now only a few weeks away and he was growing older than even he thought he would achieve.

Jack walked in to the kitchen area of the living room

and proceeded to find the essential stuff for a good Sunday morning. It was then it dawned on him there was nothing apart from a tea bags, milk and sugar; they hadn't gone shopping the day before. At least, he reasoned, he could follow his routine to the end of stage one; a big mug of tea and a joint. It was a way he had spent every Sunday morning for the past couple of decades, whether it be waking with a hangover like today or from coming home on a massive amphetamine come-down during his insane clubbing days; the mad old days of dancing until dawn on all kinds of weird uppers and alcohol, and then coming down at home on a steady diet of pot and tea.

With the kettle boiled Jack made his big mug of tea and moved over to the two-seater sofa. It was there he held court the night before, rolling joint after joint, drinking the wine and enjoying himself. Sitting down he rolled and then smoked the joint as he drank his tea. He now felt ready for the world and walking in to the bedroom he shook Clare awake to see if she wanted to come with him.

"Ah ... not now lover, my head ..." she mumbled before rolling over to bury her face in her pillow. Jack looked at her momentarily and took in the magnitude of her magnificent bum; firm and peachy it was a scene he would have to return to at the next available opportunity. He could feel the blood rushing to his dick, aware that he was getting aroused but his need for food was too great to make him hang around. Checking for keys, wallet, phone and tobacco in his pockets he headed on down the stairs.

It was a beautiful Sunday morning and the sea-air felt wonderful against his skin. Walking out on to the green that sat in the middle of their square he remembered he had seen a couple of supermarkets up on what appeared to be a main road. The square was quiet and Jack pulled the phone from his pocket; it read 08:27. It was very early by Jack's normal routine but he knew that there had to be one shop which would have open early enough just so he could get some breakfast. As he walked to the top of the square he spotted a big chain store that was open and around twenty minutes later he walked out with enough to keep himself feed for at least a week. As he walked around the shop it looked as if most of the staff and pretty much every customer were afflicted with a similar condition to Jack. It was not a good-looking scene.

Walking back to the flat Jack saw a few people sat outside a boarded-up old bank building drinking cans of very strong beer. It seemed to be a town where everyone drank, where there was always somewhere open to get a drink. Walking over the green his eyes went to the top floor flat and it still looked all quiet. Pulling the new set of keys from his jeans pocket he went back in to the block of flats and up to the flat. He walked in to the kitchen and began storing his purchases away; all apart from the coffee which he kept on the sideboard by the kettle. As the kettle began to boil again Jack moved over to one of his many boxes of belongings and pulled out three mugs. The kettle boiled and Jack mixed his and Clare's just how they liked it; he would leave Lisa's black as he had no idea how she took coffee. He supported all three in his right hand and walked across to the bedroom where, as he entered, he placed the mugs on the bedside table and proceeded to take his jeans off.

He whispered "I've got something for you baby" in

Clare's ear and saw her roll over.

"I bet you have," she replied sliding her hand down between his legs. Her hand slid over his hardening dick and a moment later they kissed. She pulled him in tight and their kissing became more passionate. Breaking apart she helped Jack out of his T-shirt before noticing the mugs set down on the cabinet. Reaching over she grabbed a mug that looked milky and drank down a good half of it before turning to Lisa, still lying sound asleep on the other side of the bed, and cajoling her to wake.

"We've got some coffee ..."

"Hmm ... uh, what? Coffee? Where?"

"Right here," Clare offered passing over the mug full of black coffee.

With no words Lisa drank it down in one mouthful.

"Wow, now I'm awake. Jack, was this your bright idea?"

He nodded and picked up his own mug, taking a decent mouthful.

"Ah, what a sweetie," Lisa announced moving over towards him. She pulled him close and kissed him. There was a passion to the kiss that suggested more than gratefulness for the coffee.

The kiss grew in passion and suddenly Clare grabbed Jack's left arm as Lisa grabbed his right. They pinned him to the bed and began placing their lips all over his chest, neck and face. Jack simply laid back and let them do whatever they wanted.

Clare pulled Lisa close and kissed her, pulling her vest top over her head. Jack closed in and let his hands slide in round Lisa's tits, sliding his fingers over her aroused nipples and kissing her neck. A groan emitted from Lisa's mouth as Clare's hands worked their way in to her friends' sexy black panties. Jack knew he should rest against the wall and pull Lisa tight and close letting his now hard dick run up the valley to her bum which was now being released by Clare who was pulling Lisa's panties down. Lisa mounted Jack's dick in reverse and suddenly Jack felt a sensation unlike anything else he'd ever experienced. His dick was deep inside a hot damp pussy and yet he could feel a tongue lapping at him as Lisa ground herself down on Clare's tongue.

The morning was spent repeating this in all manner of different combinations until finally all the sexual desire had been quenched and the three, long since naked bodies, collapsed on to the bed fulfilled at last. As the three climbed out of bed each reached for their mug of now cold coffee and began to dress from the scattered belongings on the floor.

Jack walked in to the living room and knew it was now time to get to work; there was so much to do, to get the flat looking like a home before the week of work was to commence. He grabbed the first box he came too and began working his way through it, records were leant against the wall and books and films piled high on the floor. The next box contained some things for the kitchen and then the next half-dozen were again full of records, books and films and were deposited with the rest of the collections. Clare was working her way through the three suitcases, hanging each new item of clothing on to another hanger whilst dividing the distinct underwear in to various parts of Jack's beat-up old drawer. Lisa concentrated on the kitchen and getting it all stored away properly and pondering as to what they could eat for dinner that day.

It took Jack a few hours before he finally completed the mammoth task of organising his records, books and films in to some kind of order. Clare, having finished in the bedroom some time before, and after help Lisa pick out something for dinner in the kitchen bought her box of records and books in to the living room.

Clare grabbed a couple of posters, clearly visible from one of the boxes and decided they should go up in the living room, just as Lisa walked in to announce that food was ready. Jack hadn't even thought about food yet but was grateful that at least someone was thinking about the normal day-to-day things. Clare and Jack followed Lisa and after grabbing a plate each from an open cupboard began loading up on pasta, pesto and veggie-chicken pieces along with some bread.

"Tastes great Lisa," Jack said, after devouring a few mouthfuls.

"Thanks, I thought we could do with something substantial after the work we all put in today."

~ ~ ~

With the food eaten the three moved back in to the main living room area and sat on the three seats available.

"Want to watch a movie?" Jack asked, seeing an opportunity to return to something resembling his usual routine.

They finally all agreed on some stupid modern Hollywood comedy, just the kind of film Jack loved watching on a Sunday afternoon, and settled in with Jack again designated as the chief joint roller. The afternoon passed in a blur of weed smoke and bad fart jokes and slowly turned in to a Sunday evening.

The pot made Jack drowsy enough to contemplate sleep early that night and, just after ten, he stood up and announced he was off to bed. He knew Monday was going to bring with it some problems; he had never been fond of the commute to work when he lived less than ten miles and five train stations away from work, tomorrow he would have to take two, possibly three trains over a seventy-mile route through countless stations.

NINETEEN

The alarm the next morning, despite Jack knowing it was coming, still came as a shock. He looked over at the bedside cabinet and noticed his phone, vibrating and announcing it was time for him to get out of bed; it read 06:30 and Jack wished he could remain in bed for a while longer. It wasn't to be as the alarm again sounded, announcing it was now 06:31.

Climbing out of bed his first realisation was that he had spent the night alone and that, as usual, he needed coffee, a joint and a piss but not necessarily in that order. He ran to the toilet and relieved himself before turning his attention to the kettle and the joint-rolling process. By seven he was washed, scrubbed, feed and caffeinated enough to consider himself ready for work. The ubiquitous early-morning joint had seemed to do the trick too so as he walked out the front door of his block he felt calm, relaxed and ready for the ordeal of getting to work.

The walk to the station, a mere ten minutes, went smoothly enough but then upon arrival in the waiting area Jack couldn't quite believe just how many people there were. His train was announced as being ready on platform four and due for departure in about five minutes and as Jack began to saunter over to the ticket barrier it became apparent that most of the others who had been waiting appeared to getting on his train. Too stoned to push through Jack squeezed on board regardless and was not best pleased to see not one empty seat available for him to rest on. The train ploughed through the countryside with Jack unable to see any of it due to the close confines he was caught in. It was not an ideal situation and as the train pulled in to East Croydon Jack decided to get off and change trains. Anything, he reasoned, had to be better than that.

He stood around waiting for an announcement, looking up at the time rolling around to eight-fifteen, for a train in to the centre of the city and eventually an empty train pulled in at his platform heading towards London Bridge. Jack climbed on board and as the train pushed off in the direction of its destination he realised it was the train he had got every working day for the previous five years. At his old station, the one he had left on Friday, the same people were waiting as usual and poured on as the train paused to pick them up. Jack had never talked to any of them so he continued to gaze out the window at the morning developing in the outside world; after the first journey he was just grateful to have a seat and something to look at besides the pinstripes of a business suit. As the train began its entry in to New Cross Gate train station Jack looked up and saw large UFO battle-ship firing lasers at what Jack thought was the Goldsmiths' art college. Flames were visible from the roof of the structure and Jack knew he would have to check the news when he got to work. It looked like a serious attack. The train terminated at London Bridge and Jack crossed over to platform six knowing the next train would be his last of the morning commute. Five minutes passed before he finally began the descent of the stairs at Waterloo East to street-level. Now it was just a short walk over the bridge before he'd get to work and it had always been his favourite part of his commute. It was the perfect little walk during which he could smoke one, if not two, roll-ups and properly prepare himself for work.

The days passed easily with a little more coffee on each as Jack's life feel in to some haphazard routine; he would wake, he would have a breakfast of coffee, toast with jam and if he was feeling generous a couple of supermarket brand Weetabix imitations. After devouring the food he would finish off his coffee with the first joint of the day. That first one, that even on a workday morning, can send you off to blissville where you can remain for hopefully about a half-hour. Jack would sit and contemplate as the pot took a hold of his mind what he had ahead of him that day at work. He would have a journey to work similar to his experience on Monday. On some days he found himself taking even more than the three he had that day just to escape the damn infernal crowds, the sheer mass of humanity who would constantly try to invade what little space he already had. The mornings were always a horror that was something that became clear during the first week of Jack's new commute.

Arriving at work which was, in comparison to his colleagues, a low-paid job for the amount of responsibility he had to carry on his shoulders, he would make another coffee and get to work. Pigeonholes checked, logged and delivered, more filing, an academic with an IQ of 180 not being able to work a photocopier.

"Oh Jack, do you think you could?" would come their blithering request.

What was he meant to say he thought as he took whatever it was and did the copies for a class that was due to have started some ten minutes earlier.

"Oh Jack, would you mind?"

Photocopied and delivered to the waiting class Jack would return to the office and again begin to wade through the filing before another interruption, this time to go to the archive and retrieve these files. Sometimes this would take an hour as the archive reached as far down as the basement and as high as the top floor, there were cabinets strewn throughout the building, anywhere there was space. Jack would move around the building collecting files from all points above and below his office. It would continue like this until lunchtime when he finally got a rest. He would go and sit in the staff lounge and eat his lunch whilst reading either a newspaper or a book, this week Jack had been reading *The Wild Boys*, a novel by William Burroughs that confused him a lot. He also took a few opportunities to walk outside for a nicotine fix.

After lunch he would return to work, often it was work his major boss, Diana, didn't even know he was doing.

"Student attendance, no problem, Jack can put the figures together for us."

Jack was rarely at his desk except to sort out even more filing or checking and answering e-mails or putting together more figures for more reports. There were a few people who he worked with that did a good job but there were also one or two who didn't, one in particular who got Jack to pretty much do everything for her. Jack was convinced, as were some of his colleagues, that Jackie had only got the job as she knew Diana before hand and not down to any relevant employment history or skills. This particularly annoyed another of Jack's colleagues, Pippa, who'd also applied for the job. Then eventually, around half-past-five, work would stop and it would be time to travel back home. The first week, if anything was learnt, showed him that on his evening trip before the move he had got very lucky. That night it had taken a little under an hour to reach Brighton. Now it was common for Jack to arrive home, at the earliest, just after seven. At least, he reasoned, on the train home, he generally always got a seat and a window to look out of if he couldn't be bothered with reading.

Getting home, he would immediately proceed to roll a joint and pursue the futility of trying to get Clare or Lisa to make him some food. After his joint then he would get food and not long after he would fall asleep. Thursday night he fell asleep at nine-thirty and was in bed, snoring, by ten. The journey was becoming too much for him but what was he supposed to do? He couldn't very well quit the best job he'd ever had but he could, he began to think, find a job for himself in Brighton.

Friday finally came in to view and Jack had never been so grateful at it being the end of the working week. After work and ripping his old routine to shreds, he left straight for home. That night he was home just after seven and in bed by half past. He slept for a few hours, woke, ate a baguette full of cheese, drank a beer and smoked a joint and suggested to Clare and Lisa that maybe they could go out?

The three of them hadn't spent much time together during that first week and Jack was curious to see what was out there in their new town.

"Well, you could come with Lisa and me to our new job if you want?"

"New job, but Clare ..."

"Yeah so did I but it appears the old manager doesn't want to leave so I'm now their assistant. It's a bit of a cut in my wages but then ..."

"Well, then," Lisa continued, " ...I got an offer, so to speak, from a friend of mine..."

"Do tell, you tease. What is it?" Jack asked.

"Well, I hope I can tease 'cos then I'll be getting the real big money but right now I'm just working on my routine. I got a job at a gentlemen's club, stripping, dancing, you know the sort of thing."

Whilst he had never attended one Jack had a pretty good idea of the sort of things that happened at them. It was an image built entirely in his mind with no real knowledge to back it up.

"We're due to arrive about half-eleven for a start at midnight so I better get scrubbed up and prettified," Lisa concluded walking off to the bathroom.

"You fancy coming, showing us some support?" Clare asked moving in to kiss him.

"Sure, yeah, love too" he responded before her furtive tongue darted in to his mouth to silence him. She turned and walked towards the dressing room, what would have been the third bedroom in a normal flat-share, closing the door behind her.

Jack walked in to the kitchen and looked at himself in the mirror; he didn't look like someone who dated an exotic dancer but here he was preparing to go with not one, but two, beautiful women who he'd fucked in the last week.

Ten minutes later and the three of them converged in the living room; Jack had dressed up, wearing an old leather jacket he'd got from Camden market many years before with a flowery Hawaiian shirt and black corduroy jeans and a pair of trainers. Clare walked out in a long coat that immediately looked familiar to Jack; it was what she had worn that night to the park to cover her sexy Britney style school uniform. Lisa presented herself in a pair of tight denim shorts, an even tighter T-shirt with bright multi-coloured bra underneath and finished off with a pair of black fishnet stockings, held up by a suspender belt buried under her T-shirt. She too wore a black leather jacket and a pair of trainers. Jack looked at both of them.

"Wow, don't I suddenly feel like the luckiest fucker in the world?"

They both laughed and kissed letting tongues enter mouths on both sides, Jack was beguiled.

TWENTY

As they left the flat Clare and Lisa each grabbed one of Jack's arms. The last time they'd left to go to a shift they had dressed in normal everyday clothing but the boss had told them to wear their sexiest gear for tonight.

"If you play it right on Friday night you could make a ton of money. Seriously, I know a few who've taken over a grand just for one nights work," he had said, encouraging them to get sexy for him and his customers.

Less than ten minutes later and they were walking through the door to a place called the Sapphire Lounge. On the door was a large black man by the name of Clarence; he had originally not wanted to let Jack in but when Lisa told him to speak to Oscar, the club manager, he backed down and let him enter without any further talk. The door opened directly on to a staircase that went down, it was a tight narrow passage, which at the bottom opened up to the left where a bar was located. There were a few guys sat there already and Jack made a break to join them, taking a seat and grabbing a drinks menu. Clare and Lisa disappeared off behind a curtain with a large sign on it reading 'EMPLOYEES ONLY' and guarded by a short, shaven-headed middle-aged white guy. He was wearing the same generic security outfit as Clarence and Jack noticed there were another couple, one of whom was a scarily-proportioned shaven-headed man in his early twenties, wandering the floor of the club ensuring no one did anything they weren't suppose to do. They were all wearing the same uniform; Jack felt lucky that he didn't need to wear one for work; he pretty much got away with whatever he wanted to wear. His mind turned to the drinks menu, it was long and all very expensive but fortunately Larry, the bartender, had noticed Jack walk in with Lisa and Clare, and informed him all guests get drinks half-price. Jack looked down the list. There were many he wanted but he should stick to just one type of drink tonight. It was a place where if you got silly with money it would vanish very quickly. Jack decided on a decent bottle of Belgium beer as that was strong enough to take the edge off what was unfolding to be quiet a memorable night.

There was a gorgeous woman, early twenty-something with beautiful shoulder-length blonde hair that was flayed all over the place as she performed some elaborate shapes around the pole. Jack poured the contents of the bottle in to a glass, sat back, took in the show and slowly worked his way through his first beer; at the prices he was being charged it was just like another night in a pub back in central London.

A second beer ordered and poised for consumption Jack's eyes are at last consumed by a sight even more beautiful than a bottle of Belgium beer, his girlfriend dancing on the stage in the very outfit she had worn to seduce him in the park that weird, glorious night just after they had first met, still only two short months ago, but already another city and lifetime away. It had all changed so much.

On stage Clare was proceeding to undo her blouse to

reveal a cute sports bra that clung to her impressive breasts. She wildly threw the blouse off and suddenly her short skirt is upside down and the crowd gasp at her white cotton panties, already moist with her juices. Jack had never seen her display such flexibility and knew he would have to get her to pull same shapes like that with him. With one arm hanging on to the pole the other began to rub down her thigh before stopping and momentarily stroking her panties. As a hand moved up towards her waist it dramatically undid one button on her skirt and it feel to the ground. Jack could hear the crowd moan their approval.

It was then that Lisa entered from behind the curtain at the end of the stage. She is dressed how a schoolmistress would dress in a low-budget porn movie and she is carrying a paddle. Clare it is explained has been a bad girl and needs some punishment. The pair of them put on a little show for a couple of minutes before Lisa disrobes to reveal an already naked body. The crowd gasp their approval as Lisa grabs Clare and the pair of them began kissing passionately on the podium's floor. They remain there for a few minutes, kissing and touching each other frantically, before Clare stands tall and removed her bra. Lisa's arms reach up, one rubbing a nail over Clare's left nipple whilst the right arm begins grappling at her dance partners panties. Clare's eyes close as she becomes aware of what is happening and with them both now naked they kiss and turn, rushing towards the curtain. The crowd burst in to wild applause, shouting and hollering with their delight at the show they've just witnessed.

Jack sits at the bar knowing that tonight he will fuck

both of the women who the crowd are now going wild for; it is inevitable he thinks, turning to the bar for another of those glorious beers. About halfway down the bottle, he'd given up with the pre-text of sophistication that always came with drinking from a glass. He felt his phone vibrate in his jeans front-right pocket and reached for it; it was a message from Clare. The main auditorium was only half as full as before he'd got his beer and he wondered where everyone had gone.

He entered his password and switched the tab for messages and up came her text; she was going to be really busy for the next couple of hours but she hoped he would stay and he could tab his drinks to her account. 'Of course,' he replied, 'I'll stay. Remember, you are my queen, you are everything to me!' He would do whatever it was she wanted him to do and the idea of free beer and a whole host of sexy women dancing in front of him made it an even easier decision. Jack's mind wandered off in to the Belgium beer induced ether where pure joy poured forth from him. He couldn't ever remember when he'd been so happy but something surely needed to change, starting with a new job. For the next couple of hours Jack hung out at the bar, tabbing his order to Clare who was apparently in the process of earning a couple of months rent in one night. Eventually their private shows came to an end and they returned from behind the curtain arm in arm wearing what they had walked in wearing, right down to their coats which suggested it was time for Jack to sober up and get ready for a night of insane depravity.

TWENTY-ONE

Jack woke up on Saturday morning determined not to move until he had too; his whole routine has been systematically destroyed in the course of the last week and he needed more rest. After at least ten minutes of just lying there, stock-still, Jack finally stretches his legs and arms out to wake him limbs and begin his morning routine. This had remained the only part of his day that remained unaffected; it was his bliss-time. In a life where he got to share bliss-time with two beautiful women it felt like he needed his own private time now more than ever before; it was like a connection with his old life reminding him of where he'd come from.

It had been a mad night but Jack's head felt fine that morning and that first mug of tea went down smoothly and the joint allowed him to drift off, contemplating what he could do on a day off with no hangover. He sat deliberating on this matter for a while; he smoked a couple of joints and was just contemplating brewing another mug of tea when Clare walked in to the living room.

"Morning," she greeted, prompting Jack to walk over and grab her round her waist, covered by a white vest-top that was becoming to look familiar. She always slept in a similar outfit and Jack liked the way Clare's body looked. He kissed her and stuck the kettle back on.

"Care for a cuppa something?"

"Sure, make mine a coffee if that's OK. Just like the

other morning, that was perfect."

She returned to the bedroom to get changed and re-appeared just as the kettle was coming to the boil. She'd slipped on a pair of tight blue denim jeans and a big over-sized T-shirt.

"Sit down, I'll bring them in," he called as he finished stirring her coffee.

They sat and talked about the night before. Clare told him that she could feel his eyes burning in to her during her stage-time the night before; it really turned her on knowing the effect her performance would be having on him. She told him about all that happened in her private shows and his paranoia was calmed about what could have happened when she was out of his sight.

Conversation finally turned to the flat. It looked OK but there was still some stuff that needed fixing up they concluded. It was then Jack suddenly realised it was Saturday afternoon and football was imminent. Lisa walked in to the kitchen in a simple white bra and panties and began to boil the kettle. She wanted a mug of coffee to ease the head that was currently imploding on top of her neck. Jack went over to the sofa where his laptop sat, grabbed it and sat down in its place, powering it up as he got settled. The desktop went through its start-up and pretty soon Jack was clicking on the Internet logo and he was online.

Lisa walked in the main living-room area and sat down next to Clare.

"It's Saturday so Jack's going to be unsociable all afternoon reading about some football nonsense. You fancy doing something? Maybe a bit of shopping, get some stuff for this flat with our takings from last night, maybe?"

"Sure," Lisa replied without hesitation, " ...just let me get my head straight first."

"About an hour you reckon?" Clare asked.

"Sure, that sounds about right. I just need some coffee, a few roll-ups and a wash and I'll be fine."

~ ~ ~

Jack settled in to his seat and thus his routine, despite feeling Lisa's eyes stare at him almost, seemingly, pleading with him to stop what he was doing. He didn't care right now, it was a Saturday afternoon and all he cared about was finding the Millwall commentary page. As he watched the team load he suddenly remembered a feeling that was common to his old life; the nervous energy of a Saturday afternoon.

Lisa came too pretty quickly and by two forty-five she and Clare were out the flat and Jack was alone. It was just like his old life except the flat was much nicer, much bigger and with a fantastic view.

The afternoon's events unfolded in dramatic fashion; unbelievably Millwall took an early and then commanding lead away against a team they shared an arch-rivalry with; it had nothing to do with locality, it was one of sheer hatred built on equal baiting of both of clubs support in the tabloid press. Leeds United, at the Den, was sure to get tasty with various ill-considered chants launched in our direction with increasing ferocity by Yorkshire men displaying all the signs of heart-attack symptoms and a huge amount of police on overtime. This season it was sure to be a nothing match on the pitch as both teams have struggled for mediocrity and were wallowing in the bottom half, already worrying about that day in May when the season would end and where they would be in the table. Today, however, with his team already three-nil up and it only being half-time he felt it a good time for an early drink. It was a good day to be a Millwall fan and during years like these Jack knew to seize every single one of them. He surveyed the kitchen and spots a bottle of wine, and after checking the fridge for a beer only to discover none, goes to open it. There is only half-bottle left but Jack's thirst must be quenched somehow so he pops the cork out and begins pouring before he's even really aware of what he is doing. Seconds later the bottle stands empty and Jack is back, laptop in place just in time for the second-half to begin. The second-half seems to revolve around them trying to break through our midfield and not succeeding; it is a display of futility as we attempt to merely keep the ball away from our goal. An epic display of attrition, the kind of football you won't see on Match of the Day. As the game ends on the laptop Jack shows delight that had been blustered by its inevitability during the second-half. His right arm swoops down and picks up his half-glass of red wine that has been sat on the floor.

With the game over Jack decides to roll a monster joint to compensate for the inadequate amount of alcohol on offer. With the joint rolled he hears a couple of giggling voices outside the front door and the sound of a set of keys being slide in the lock. Clare and Lisa stumble in and head immediately for the kitchen, they've been drinking.

'I'm in the clear' Jack thinks, downing his glass of wine and sparking the joint that he is struggling to support with his mouth. He tokes firmly on it a couple of times before flicking the remnants in to the nearby ashtray. Checking that it is properly ablaze Jack takes a big long lungful of smoke and, pausing, lets his mind unleash. As he staggers to his feet he walks in to the kitchen and the first thing he hears is Clare's voice.

"What the hell is that?" he hears her ask.

"What?" Jack asks opening his eyes to take in the scene.

"That thing in your hand" Lisa asks, emphasizing where he should be concentrating.

"Oh this," he says, laughing and waving it around in front of his face, "Why, you want some?"

"Sure I do," Lisa instantly replies moving to grab it from his hand.

"Wait, patience ..." he says taking another epic toke on the beast of a joint before passing it over.

The three of them move in to the living room and Jack re-takes his place on his armchair. Lisa takes a couple more tokes before passing it to Clare who, after one toke, looks scared as she walks over to Jack, joint pointing out in front of her and towards him. Jack and Lisa, and then eventually Clare again, smoke the remainder of the joint and kickback, relaxing for the next couple of hours. It is beautiful moment of bliss-time out of the bedroom and shared by the three of them.

Later as they come too from their mutual haze Clare moves over and begins to kiss Jack. She ensures he remains seated as she puts on a little show akin to one she gave last night but with a few additional treats for her boyfriend. Her short skirt barely covers her bum as she glides it down in to his groin, slowly beginning to grind whilst lifting the blue denim material up to uncover a pair of black lace panties. Feeling her grind down Jack can feel her ass cheeks open as his dick grows hard inside his jeans. She stands up, spins round and is down on the floor in a flash. Her hands go up to his waist and begin to undo his belt buckle and then the buttons that hold his jeans closed. His dick suddenly jumps to attention and she slides her bum firm up against his groin, pushing his dick back just as his hands reach round to her waist, pulling at her panties. Lisa suddenly comes too and immediately moves towards the pair of them, taking her top off and sliding a hand up her skirt before positioning her tongue deep inside Clare's pussy, finally helping Jack slide her panties off. Jack stands up with Lisa slavering over Clare's wet pussy and positions his dick just by her mouth desperate for her to take him. She sees what he is trying to do and fulfils his desire by taking him deep inside her mouth; she has never quite felt this turned on with a woman's tongue in her pussy and a big fat dick in her mouth; she is in wonderland. Waves of euphoria pour through her as she is hit by a multitude of orgasms, covering Lisa with her ejaculate. After a few more hours in various positions and combinations the three of them collapse in a heap, finally having vanquished all sense of tension. They all sleep well that night.

TWENTY-TWO

Waking earlier than was usual for a Sunday Jack's mind was still engulfed with images from the previous nights' fun even before he looked over at Clare and Lisa, lying naked and asleep on the bed beside him. Lisa was face-up and Jack took in the magnificent sight of her breasts, in fact her whole body was a pretty great image. Her legs were shapely despite being quite short and her pussy looked good enough to eat but Jack felt he'd had too good a time the night before to sate any further desire in that direction. Her stomach was flat and quite tight rising up to her magnificent breasts, which then just cried out to be touched. Rounding it all off with that beautiful naturally dark hair and angelic face with its cute nose and a mouth that looked built for pleasure Jack felt a huge smile grow across his face. Finished off with a pair of brown eyes that looked as if they could stop a train at full speed in its tracks she was perhaps even more beautiful than Clare.

Jack climbed up off the bed, found a pair of clean boxer shorts from the room down the corridor and pulled them on as he walked in to the kitchen. He went through his morning ritual before realising that it was a Sunday and Millwall had won yesterday, it was time to go out for a newspaper. It was a ritual he went through every time Millwall won; this season it had become a rare treat as they had generally been useless Three months into the season and this would be only the second time he'd got a Sunday paper.

By the time of his return Clare and Lisa were awake and breakfast was in full swing. They were loading up the toaster and boiling water for coffee. Jack was a little surprised to see them both fully dressed; it was a rare thing to see them in such attire around the flat. Lisa, in particular, looked very fine wearing a medium length skirt with a pair of fishnets covering her legs and a tight T-shirt with a work-shirt over the top. With greetings acknowledged Jack was pleased when Clare offered him some toast and a mug of coffee.

"Thanks sweets, you good today?"

"Yeah, it's all good. Can't quite believe what we got up to last night though, how was it for you?"

"Are you serious? It was incredible, a night I shall remember forever, spent with my queen and her lover. It really was like a dream."

Breakfast passed with Jack ensconced in the newspaper and Clare and Lisa sharing the other parts of the massive broadsheet he'd bought for them all. Clare was flicking through the News section, aghast at some of the weird things going on in the world, whilst Lisa waded through the Review section.

"Here, listen to this ..." Clare announced, getting both of their attention, "... a man was found hobbling down a road near Leeds yesterday after having his genitals hacked off. They reckon the poor guy was in a state of shock."

"Well, trust me on this, any guy without his member would inevitably be shocked. Does it say how it happened?"

"No, just that he was discovered in the early hours and was immediately rushed to hospital."

"Wouldn't surprise me if it had something to do with those damn aliens ..." Jack surmised.

"Yeah, sounds like he was someone they experimented on," Clare agreed.

Jack went back to the sports section. There was a big report covering the game, it focused more on what happened in the stands than on the pitch and Jack was glad to read that the home fans behaved impeccably. After a couple of hours during which they swapped sections Jack thought it about time to think about some food again.

It was agreed that Jack would prepare them something and he promptly vanished in to the kitchen and began preparing a huge feast of spaghetti, garlic bread, veggie mince all smothered in a lovely tomato sauce. When he found a couple of bottles of red wine languishing in a kitchen cupboard he had forgotten to check yesterday he knew it would all be good and lunch was finished off with a flourish of joy.

With the afternoon fully upon them and no plans Jack suggested they watch a film; something funny, something stupid, something ideal for a lazy Sunday afternoon. He allowed Clare and Lisa to go pick something from his collection; Jack owned nearly two hundred films so they had plenty to choose from and they wisely picked out the stupid but hysterical Pink Panther box-set that was sat on the top shelf of one of his two units, stacked full of all his books, films and music. Jack had always loved watching films, reading books or listening to music but it was something that the three of them had yet to do much and he enjoyed the quiet time punctuated by bouts of hysterical laughter often bought on by the frenzied karate routines played out by Clouseau and Kato on screen in front of them. Jack must have watched the scene were Kato attacks Clouseau from within the depths of a fridge freezer maybe a hundred times but it still never failed to make him wail with hysterical laughter. When the film ended Jack was at last completely relaxed and contented, for the first time he felt at home in their new flat.

"Shall we watch another?" Clare asked.

"How about we go out and get a few beers somewhere?" Jack suggested.

"A drink, hmmm ... sounds good to me," Lisa concurred, " ...but where shall we go?"

"I don't know, somewhere with some rock 'n' roll music maybe?" Jack suggested.

"Oh, I know the perfect place. A rum bar over in Kemp Town; you'll love it!" she excitedly announced.

"Sounds good, give us about ten minutes to get ready and we can go," Clare opined.

"No need to rush baby he said walking over to the racks of shelving where his music collection sat. He knew immediately what he wanted; Pussy Galore's glorious ode to the Blaxploitation genre *Dial M for Motherfucker*.

He slid the CD in to the player and walked back to his armchair, sat and began rolling a joint. Twenty minutes later and everyone was ready. Jack had heard Dick Johnson and had smoked a joint whilst Clare and Lisa had added yet more beautification to their appearance. They both looked simply stunning and Jack would have been envious of any man walking in to a pub he was frequented with just one of them, let alone both. He knew it was going to be a good night even if a Sunday would mean it would have to be a relatively early one.

The bar was everything Lisa had promised, a huge stock of dark rum as well as numerous ales, lagers and other spirits and a DJ playing some very obscure but nevertheless fantastic rock 'n' roll, garage fuelled psychedelia and some real cool blues of the non-electric variety. What made it even better was how quiet the bar was; no more than a dozen people were sat around when the three made their entry and took up a place at the bar. Jack ordered beers for all of them and picked up what turned out to be a rum menu; it wasn't long before he stumbled across the 'specials' page and it was with delight he discovered that you could order three for only five pounds if you picked from that specific list.

"How about it?" he asked Lisa, who he thought had always displayed more hedonistic tendencies than Clare.

"Sounds good but I ain't heard of any of them. I do like dark rum though."

"Clare, are you in?" Jack asked before calling the barman back over.

"Sure, something light though for me ..."

Three different dark rums came over and Jack swiftly dispatched his in one gulp; it tasted sweet but strong and Jack knew he had to have another one.

"Same again," he announced to the barman. The evening continued like this for another forty-five minutes; Jack ordering more and more dark rum and Lisa struggling to keep up whilst Clare was still nursing what was her second. Jack had drank six by the time he realised he needed to go and visit the toilet. As he stood Clare asked if he fancied another beer, just to slow down for a while. Jack agreed before wandering off to go find the toilet.

Standing up to relieve himself he couldn't quite believe his eyes when he saw Lisa, who had somehow beaten him down the stairs, stood at the doorway to the toilet. She quickly moved towards him, pushing him back in to the more private cubicle.

"I want you Jack," she moaned as her lips moved in to kiss him. He said nothing but allowed her to kiss him passionately before moving down to take his already hard dick in her mouth. He couldn't quite believe what was unfolding and it wasn't long before he was overwhelmed by an orgasm that filled Lisa's mouth. The toilet was still empty and Jack suggested Lisa leave first, he would see her back at the bar.

With a mouthful of Jack's ejaculate Lisa went in to the ladies toilet to clean up. She couldn't believe what she had just done; Clare was falling in love with this guy and she was meant to be her best friend but there was just something about Jack that she liked a lot.

Clare was still sat at the bar, unbelievably alone until Jack's return, guarding the drinks and wondering where her friend and lover had gone. Jack walked over, kissed her and asked her where Lisa was.

"She had to go off to the toilet but that was a while ago now though, she shouldn't have taken this long unless there was a queue."

"Oh, I think I did see some people waiting down there as I left the gents. It's always the same" he said drawing on decades of experience of drinking in small pubs like this. He supped at his beer and looked, basked, in the presence of Clare, his beautiful girlfriend, whose friend he'd just allowed to suck his dick. Lisa returned and they drank another couple of rounds; it was getting late if Jack was going to make it to work the next morning. Monday was always the most hellish of commutes but was always compounded with the effects of a hangover brewing in his head. They left the pub at ten-fifty and Jack immediately began looking forward to the seven hours he was destined to get; that was never enough, Jack craved sleep, often sleeping for more than half-a-day on weekends. Jack speed off with Clare and Lisa struggling to keep up and for once he was pleased of the quiet.

Back at the flat Jack went through his pre-bed routine; a strong joint, not really needed that evening due to the quantities of dark rum he had consumed, and then sleep would come easily. It wasn't meant to be however as Jack, already down to his boxer shorts and T-shirt and sat in, what was turning in to his seat, the arm-chair and half-way through rolling the joint, caught Lisa and Clare bickering about something as they came through the door. Jack decided to concentrate on the joint in progress as he finally inhaled the first deep toke of its bliss.

"Jack," Clare said, walking over towards him.

"Yes ..."

"Lisa's told me. She told me about the two of you, how could you do this to me?"

Jack looked at Lisa and his eyes focused all his bad feeling towards her.

"Did she really tell you what happened?"

"Yes ..."

"Did she tell you she walked in on me, did she tell you it was her who pushed me in to the private cubicle, and did she tell you that it was her mouth that sucked my dick?"

"Yes, but she said you enjoyed it?"

"Of course I did, look at her; she's just as beautiful as you!"

Clare composed herself and then asked who got to sleep with him that night. Jack said that maybe it would be a good idea if Clare spent some time with Lisa so Jack could get a bit of rest and the three parted waves; Jack left the remainder of the joint with Lisa and went off to bed. He knew there was a half-smoked one from the night before lying in the ashtray nearby so he would smoke that before sleep took him in its warm embrace.

Jack fell asleep within five minutes of finishing his joint but was soon awakened by loud voices coming from the living room. He decided to try and ignore them and continue his much needed sleep. It took him no time at all to fall back asleep and it was another couple of hours before he was disturbed again. He could feel the arm of a woman stretch round to hold his chest before pulling herself in close. After what had happened earlier, in the bar, he was unsure of who he would face if he decided to roll over. It was a situation he didn't want to face up too, not now, not so soon to his dreaded alarm bell. He could feel her crotch grind its pubic bush against his bum and it felt scintillating and he knew his plan was shot to hell. It felt like a bolt of electricity pulsed through his entire body; next he felt a pair of magnificent breasts rub gently against his back and he knew. He knew it was Lisa, only she could make him feel like this and as he turned he pulled her close kissing her passionately.

"Where's Clare?"

"She's sulking in the other bedroom. Do you mind?"

"Any other night and I'd be all over you but tonight I need my sleep. I got a long week at work which I have to be awake for in less than four hours ..."

"Screw work," she said, moving her head down to his hardening dick for the second time that night. Once he was hard she leant up and told him that she wanted him to screw her. He knew then that there was no way he was going to make it to work later that morning.

TWENTY-THREE

With work ceasing to be an option Jack slept in late the next morning after his night of fucking with Lisa had reached its conclusion around the time he was due to wake up. He walked in to the kitchen and turned on the radio at the same time as the kettle. The news announcer said it was eleven and today's top story was the destruction of the famous West Pier in his new town by an alien warship. Jack knew immediately what he would say to work when he called in and after the kettle boiled he pulled his phone from his pocket. Speed-dialling the number he braced himself; their reaction was key, only then would he know if he'd pulled off the lie that was developing in his mind.

"Tina, oh hi, it's Jack. Look, did you hear about what happened last night? Well, we were evacuated and I've only just been let back in my flat. If you want me to come in I could but I didn't get much sleep last night, it all kicked off about half-one and we were evacuated in our night-clothes just before two."

"Yeah, yeah I'll be in tomorrow no problem, bar any more freaky alien activity!" and with that he hung up the phone. It was that easy, Jack almost felt as if she hadn't cared if he went in to work or not that day and so he was off the hook. He was free to spend the day doing what he liked but first of all he knew he had to look out the window of the living room, mug of tea in hand. After contemplating the scene of destruction outside his flat window he went back to his seat only then realising that Clare must be out at work and Lisa and him were alone.

An hour or so later she walked from the bedroom to the kitchen, naked as nature intended, to make herself a mug of something hot.

"I'm making some coffee, you fancy some ... lover?"

"Sure," Jack replied unsure how to read the pause in her speech before the word 'lover'. She had never called him that before but he liked the way it sounded.

Bringing two mugs full to the brim of milky coffee in to the living room she'd slipped on a T-shirt she'd found on the floor in the kitchen. Jack thought that she still looked beautiful and as she passed him a mug he reached out and pulled her in close so they could kiss. She placed her mug next to his and they became entwined again, kissing passionately. As silence filled the room Jack began to roll a joint, the second of his day but the first he'd shared. They zoned out in some mutual bliss-time and it felt really good.

~ ~ ~

When Clare arrived home, just after five-thirty, she immediately made for the kitchen but Jack is happy to think that she looks a bit perkier than expected after everything that had happened in the last twenty-four hours.

"Dinner?" she suggests, walking in to the living room and greeting Jack and Lisa.

"Sure, what do you suggest?" Jack enquired glad at the change in her mood.

"Well that old cow whose job I was meant to get finally

gave up today, so the jobs mine. I can quit the dancing job, isn't that great?"

The silence is deafening and Clare looks confused at how her good news is received. Jack feels thwarted and Lisa feels patronised but nothing is said until Clare makes a suggestion.

"Well how about we treat ourselves to a really good Chinese take-away or dinner out somewhere? It'll be my treat."

With that Jack perks up. "Great, sounds pretty fantastic honey, if memory serves me correctly the road at the top of the square was full of restaurants. One of them has got to be a good Chinese."

"Excellent," Clare agrees and finally Lisa and Jack stand up and the three head back towards the door.

The food is fantastic and Jack swigs down a couple of strong Chinese beers as he devours his kung-po hot chilli prawns on a base of egg fried rice. Once dinner is complete the three return back to the flat and things return to normal; there will be no arguments tonight. They settle in for another film, this time a weird David Lynch one called *The Lost Highway*. Within half-hour of the start Jack is completely confused but loves the way the film looks even if he has no real idea of what is going on plot-wise. That night, sleep comes easily as Jack sleeps by himself whilst Lisa and Clare share the second bedroom. Jack's alarm goes off the next morning at seven and he bounds up out of bed; by half-seven he is out the front door on his way to the train station.

On his way to work that day he receives a text message from Frank. He wants to know how Jack is doing, what's going on with him in Brighton and whether he has any plans for his birthday. With everything that Jack had been through in the past two-and-half months he'd almost forgotten it was now only a few weeks to his birthday; maybe he could have a party, let his London friends see where he lived the dream as they all thought he did.

TWENTY-FOUR

Jack arrived at work and everyone was pleased to see him return; he was less than happy to discover how much work he had to catch up on from his one day off. It seemed like a lot and he had to spend lunchtime at his desk, eating his lunch, whilst continuing to wade through the filing that had piled up. By half-past-five Jack was pleased to get out and get back on the commute home.

When he arrived back at the flat just after seven Jack was pleased to see Lisa and Clare sitting around sharing a joint; the situation from Sunday night seemed to have been completely forgotten about. Jack follows Clare's example from the previous night and suggests "dinner?" as he's handed the remnants of the joint that is now reaching the end of its passage. He takes a long hard toke and the joint smokes all the way down to the roach. He leans over, suggesting that another be rolled, and puts it out in the ashtray. Lisa begins to roll as Clare and Jack chat about options for dinner.

After smoking another joint Jack's mind can't really focus on anything beyond pizza. He finds a menu from a nearby delivery place and scans it quickly, the veggie hot seems the best option for him and on a special offer they could get three of the same size for only twenty pound. With the order confirmed and delivery estimated for half-hour Jack rolls a fresh joint and starts wondering what film they could watch that night. He soon decides on an old indie classic of his youth, a film that neither Lisa nor Clare had seen before, *Slacker*, the first Richard Linklater movie. With the pizza and joint devoured with equal zeal Jack starts the film; the next couple of hours pass in a blur of weed smoke. The mood reflects the strangeness of the movie and by the close Jack is almost ready for bed. It is a little after ten but regardless of this Jack saunters off for another quiet night.

~ ~ ~

The next morning Jack wakes early and outside it seems like it is still nighttime but according to Jack's clock he still only has forty-five minutes before he needs to leave. He drinks his coffee, smokes a joint and eats some toast before leaving for work whilst Lisa and Clare are still in bed.

Work goes smoothly and Jack gets the chance to tell Kerry about his plans for a birthday, flat-warming affair. She is happy to accept his invite and is pleased even more when Jack says she is welcome to crash in their spare room if she wants although she probably wouldn't be the only one. That would be four people from London, more than enough, who would all be staying over after the party. He hoped there would be no bad vibrations, as there had occasionally been, between the four as bar Clare and Lisa he would know no one else there. It was going to be an interesting night that was for sure.

Arriving back at the flat, unbelievably early, at just past half-six Jack is delighted to see that Clare and Lisa are preparing dinner. Clare turns as he walks in to the kitchen, taking his coat off and placing it on the back of a chair they pulled off a skip on a scavenger hunt the other week, "Hey, you're early! Welcome home ..."

"Evening," Jack meekly replies, suddenly feeling a wave of tiredness consuming his body.

"We thought, well ... it hasn't been good this week between the three of us, what with the situation, you know ... so we thought we'd cook you a dinner and show you a good time tonight" Clare suggests.

"We thought we'd start with a great stir-fry and then maybe get busy in every room in the flat, sound good?" Lisa asks spinning round and displaying a very sexy set of stockings, panties and bra underneath her pinafore. With that prompt delivered Clare moves towards Jack and tells him to sit down. Seconds later she is grinding her bum in to his groin and Jack feels himself growing hard.

That night everything is put to rest; all tensions are released as the three of them move from the kitchen to the living room to the first bedroom. Whilst Jack is fucking Lisa, who is leaning forward, naked, on the front window he can see a man walking his dog in the square. He suddenly sees the dog-walker notice them and stop, taking in the view. This appears to turn Lisa on even more once she realises she is the subject of his voyeuristic fantasies. A matter of minutes later she is overcome by a wave of euphoric orgasm, which leads him to collapse on the floor, a spent force. With Lisa in a state of recovery Jack turns his attention to Clare who, during the show, had been sitting on the two-seater sofa with her hands between her legs, getting her pussy as turned-on as she could, ready for Jack.

TWENTY-FIVE

The next morning, Thursday, Jack wakes early despite his night of pretty unrestrained pleasure seeking and immediately walks to the living room. With just a pair of boxer shorts and T-shirt on Jack pulls the long curtains open to take in the view. Again it looks like the middle of the night and Jack concludes, rather sadly, that it is going to look like this for the next five months, until spring arrives.

Arriving at work with images from last night still dominating his thoughts Jack brews a very strong mug of coffee, drinks some and smokes a roll-up, before getting on with his work. The filing has reached nightmarish levels but by lunchtime and, for once, with no interruptions Jack is almost up-to-date with the archive filing. By the end of the day he has completed nearly half his current student filing, leaving the pile looking a lot more manageable and possibly something that he could, for the first time since he'd got the job, complete the following day.

That night the three lovers spend their time watching a series of mindlessly funny teenager films picked by Jack whilst they smoke a whole heap of pot. There are laughs, there are embarrassed recollections of their own teenage years and most tellingly of all Clare and Lisa sit on the two-seater whilst Jack sits, alone, on his armchair. Sitting alone in a room full of women reminds him of the year he spent in a local girls' school during which he was working towards his A levels. In reflection it probably didn't help his concentration, and therefore his grades, having to share a classroom with a group of hormonal teenage girls. That night when the films come to an end they all go to sleep in the same bed and things seem, to Jack at least, to have returned to some semblance of normality.

Friday fly's by and Jack decides to go for a drink with Kerry to celebrate the completion of the filing and catch-up on what's been going on. It is a good way to end the week at work and Jack is pleased to miss the rush-hour; the few beers he drinks help make the train journey home even more easily navigated.

That night Lisa has work at the gentlemen's club and Clare asks Jack if he'd come along again, to support her if they had any problems with her quitting. This time Clarence, the security guard on the club's front door, has no problem with allowing Jack entry and the three crash through the queue. All the men's eyes are on Lisa and Clare thinking how these two finished up with that horrible looking middle-aged guy. Jack revels in the attention his lovers are attracting and makes a real play of walking down the narrow stair-way with Lisa on one arm and Clare on the other. Walking in to the main bar area Jack acknowledges the bartender who lines up a beer and three shots of dark rum for the group as they walk over. Lisa downs her shot and walks off, vanishing behind the 'Employees only' curtain, to prepare for her show. Clare and Jack sit at the bar taking in the scene. It is then that Oscar, the club's manager, spots one of his star dancers sat at the bar.

"Hey Clare," he swoons walking towards the pair.

"Oh hi Oscar, how's it going?" she asks.

"Better now you're here. Are you ready to dance for me?"

"Oh not tonight Oscar; I'm only here to quit and support Lisa. I got the job I thought I was going to get so I don't need to dance anymore."

"Ah, that's too bad Clare; it's rare we get someone as good as you through our doors. Is there no way I can persuade you to change your mind?"

"Thanks Oscar but no, there is nothing you can say ... I have made my decision."

"Too bad, you could have made so much money."

"It ain't all about the money for me ..." she replied putting to an end any hope Oscar may have held.

That night Clare was just one of the crowd and she loved it; watching the sexy women on stage gyrating and stripping as if just for her and Jack. By two she is squirming in her seat, feeling that all too familiar horny sensation between her thighs.

"I need to get out of here," she whispers in Jack's ear as Lisa leaves the stage. She has just put on a great sexy show that has left Jack with a rock-hard dick struggling to remain encased in his boxer shorts.

"OK, shall we wait for Lisa?"

"No, I need this now ... I can't wait any longer ..."

Leaving the club the streets are practically deserted and despite their flat being less than ten minutes away Jack knows that when Clare wants it like she wants it now, she needs it immediately. She drags him off to a nearby car park and the pair fucks like a pair of desperate teenagers with nowhere better to go. Less than half-hour later however and they are walking back towards their flat, passing the club where Clarence tells them Lisa has just left. The pair begin to run, hoping to catch-up with her but by the time they reach their house-door they are still alone.

Lisa is asleep in the main bedroom by the time they walk through their front door and not long after the pair of them joins her. Jack is awoken the next morning with the sensation that someone is sucking on his dick and, after pulling the sheets back, is pleased to see it is Lisa's mouth giving him some attention. The three of them spend the rest of the morning playing around until, around lunchtime, Jack realises it is a Saturday.

Walking in to the kitchen Jack begins his routine; tea, toast, joint, laptop, joint, tea and hopefully another victory for Millwall. He loses the afternoon in a blur of weed smoke as the football becomes the centre of his universe for a couple of hours. The game that day against fellow strugglers Yeovil at The Den should, and probably would in any other season, mean three pretty easy points. Today however it seems the team have forgotten how to score, wasting several clear-cut chances before finally succumbing to what almost felt like an inevitable one-nil defeat. It was the one shot on target their opponents could muster and that just seems to be all too common this season. Yet again the team have contrived to lose a game they dominated and should have won with ease.

With the game over Jack goes through his post-match routine; joint, contemplations on dinner, joint, a glass of wine whilst dinner is being cooked, then finish the bottle after dinner with a couple more joints. Then it would be time to go out; where could they go? He wasn't in London now and his local may now be just around the corner but he has no idea what it is like. 'Perhaps,' he thinks, 'tonight we should find out?'

Standing up from his armchair he navigates his way to the kitchen where he discovers Lisa and Clare cooking up some food, having clearly been shopping again as a couple of bottles of new red wine sit on the table. Grabbing one of them he tugs at the wrapper covering the cork before taking three wine glasses off the nearby shelf. As he pours out three large glassfuls of wine he turns his attention to Lisa and Clare.

"I was thinking tonight we could go to a pub? Lisa, any suggestions as to where we could go for some wild rock 'n' roll music, some inexpensive beer and a decent crowd?"

"Well, how about that rum bar over in Kemp Town?" Lisa suggests.

"Somewhere different, somewhere new for Clare and me" Jack retorts.

"Hmm, well let me think it over whilst we eat dinner."

During dinner Lisa fires questions at the pair about what sort of place they would all enjoy. It turns out one of the problems of living in a town with so many good bars are there are just too many to choose from; a rare problem indeed in a nation where pubs are closing down every day.

"I just need to check something, is it alright if I use your laptop Jack?" Lisa asks as she finishes off her plate before chucking it in the sink.

"Sure it is, anytime" he replies as Lisa leaves the kitchen moving towards Jacks' seat in the living room.

Clare and Jack soon finish up and go in to join her. Clare sits on the arm of the chair as Jack moves over to his music system and digs out an old piece of vinyl. The Sonics *Here Are ...* album revs into action as he prepares another joint.

"Oh great, it's on ...." Lisa proclaims after a few minutes of digging around the Internet.

"What?" Clare asks.

"Yes, what!" Jack emphasizes.

"A friend of mine is having a party, we could go to that!"

"Great, is it nearby?"

"They live in a flat up near Seven Dials, so maybe a twenty-minute walk uphill. On the upside when we're drunk later and coming home it'll be all down-hill."

"Sounds good ..." Jack and Clare echo in unison.

The joint passes round and with the party not due to start until about eleven and the living-room clock saying it was still only nine Jack, again, reverts to type.

"How about we go to a pub before the party?"

"Yeah, OK but there aren't too many good pubs up that way? Just a lot of locals only types with huge screens for Sky Sports or those hipster micro-brew bars."

"You know about the pub round the corner?"

"All I know about that place is it is meant to be very odd; strange beer, strange prices, strange customers ..."

"Sounds interesting, want to go there for a couple?" Jack suggests.

"We could I suppose, I've never been inside but it even looks a bit weird from the outside so who knows, maybe it'll be a treat, a hidden gem."

Preparing themselves for the party takes about half-hour, Jack takes about thirty seconds before sitting down in his armchair rolling another joint whilst working out how much he should take to the party. By the time they are ready to leave both Lisa and Clare look stunning whilst Jack is just a little bit more stoned. He again feels like the luckiest man alive.

Lisa walks out first; wearing a tight Ramones T-shirt and leather-jacket coupled with a short denim skirt, tights and those old Chuck Taylor imitation trainers. Clare follows, an old denim-jacket covering a long plaid shirt that stretches down to her knees, with a belt around the waist, a pair of tights and a big old pair of boots. Jack is resplendent in a pair of black cords, a pair of trainers similar to Lisa's except hers are red whilst his are black, a T-shirt hidden under a plaid shirt and a light brown windbreaker jacket.

When the three walk in to the odd little bar around the corner Jack feels like a Clint Eastwood-type in an old western; there is a silence and it seems everyone in the place turns to look at them. Lisa and Clare pull up a couple of seats at the bar and Jack attempts to negotiate with the bartender.

"I'll need to check their ID's before I serve anyone," he demands.

"ID?" he checks before turning to Lisa and Clare, "got any ID?"

"Really?" Lisa asks, aghast that a woman in her late twenties could still be asked to provide such evidence before buying a drink. The pair begin to hunt throw their purses.

"No," Lisa replies first.

"I got my old provisional drivers' licence," Clare offers.

"If your friend ain't got any I can't serve any of you," the barman retorts, seemingly happy that they will have to leave.

"But I'm twenty-eight years old; I haven't been asked to present ID for nearly five years."

"Don't matter; no ID, no drink."

"Fucking ridiculous," Lisa seethes grabbing her jacket off the back of her chair.

Jack turns from the bar and the three of them make to leave.

"I can't believe that, what was his fucking problem?" Jack angrily asks as they walk from the pub.

"Fuck knows, I did tell you it was a weird bar."

"Now I really need a drink. Let's just go in the first one we find ... I don't care right now," Jack suggests.

Despite this the next pub has loud disco music blasting from it so they continue to walk, growing increasingly desperate, before finally finding somewhere that looks like they could get a drink.

The three walk in and no one bats an eye-lid, all is calm and no one pays any attention to them as they pull up three seats at the bar. Jack gesticulates to the bartender that they require service and moments later Jack has downed his first shot of dark rum and is starting on his first pint. Lisa and Clare are sharing a bottle of red wine. No one talks to them or even makes eye contact as they sit there finishing their drinks before ordering some more.

"It's almost eleven," Lisa announces as Jack gets to the lower echelons of his second pint.

"Cool," Clare responds, " ...you know where we are going don't you?"

"Yep, I've even got the address stored in my phone and a map to tell us how to get there. It should be about another ten minutes from here."

Jack finished his pint, stood to his feet and asks, "Well, shall we?"

The three stand and walk out the door. It was a weird little place but Jack had already ruled it out as a place to hang out regularly. 'There has to be a local bar that is good,' he thought as the three of them turned up the hill and continued the walk to the party.

When they arrive the party is slowly warming-up. Lisa inevitably leads the way, hoping that she recognises somebody to announce their arrival too. It is a big flat with multiple rooms of which it appears at least two are bedrooms.

"How many people live here Lisa?" Jack enquires upon realising that they've just dumped their coats in what transpires to be the second bedroom of three.

"It's only Toby and Julie, they've got a load of space haven't they?"

"They sure have, I've lived in rooms smaller than that bathroom!"

Walking from the second bedroom to the living room Lisa finally sees Julie and waves excitedly at her. Julie reciprocates and moves over towards the group. Introductions are made and the group trail off to the main bedroom where Jack takes up the offer of a seat and the opportunity to roll a joint. He sits back, relaxes and commences the whole business of assembling a joint for more than four people. By the time he finishes it is nearly six-inches long and has employed a few rolling papers. As Jack sits back upon completing his task he grinds the roach of the joint in between his teeth and lights. Lisa looks over at Jack and applauds and giggles wildly.

"I told you Julie, he's a good one!" Jack hears her say.

The joint makes it round the group once before Toby finally shows his face. He is grateful to have arrived mid-joint and eagerly tokes when it's offered, repaying Jack with half a bottle of red wine. Jack slugs it down as Toby gets high and as Toby finally finishes the joint a loud banging noise comes screaming through from the living room. Toby stands up demanding to know, "What the hell is that racket?"

"Think it might be ..." Julie begins to suggest before Toby storms off. He clearly doesn't care for what she thinks he just wants the horrible noise to stop.

As he walks in to the living-room Toby moves over to the computer from which the music is streaming and notices that someone has moved away from his pre-designed playlist for the night. It was a playlist that had taken him the best part of a lifetime to develop and then the best part of a week to put together and the room immediately calms upon hearing the familiar strains of Spiritualized fill the room.

The party goes on for a few more hours but eventually Jack and Clare have had enough; they want to get out and go home to sleep. Jack goes to look for Lisa whilst Clare says good-bye to all the guests who are still partying.

After searching the two bedrooms and the living room Jack still couldn't find Lisa and Clare becomes worried that she's left with someone else.

"Before we go, I better take a pee ..." Jack says moving

towards the bathroom. The door is locked so he knocks. There is no reply and Jack persuades Clare to go find out if there is a key. He again hammers on the door as Clare walks off.

"I won't be long," a female voice announces from behind the door.

"Lisa, is that you?"

"Is that you Jack?"

"Yeah, what's going on?"

Behind the door silence falls and Jack walks off to find Clare to tell her of the latest developments. He is now desperate for a piss and decides to take things in to his own hands. Just as he's decided to go and piss outside the bathroom door swings open. Lisa staggers through, pulling clothes in to place, before noticing that her two friends have noticed what's going on. Jack pushes through, past some random guy, and finally gets his wish.

Clare seems angry that Lisa has been with a man and as Jack stands he can hear their voices begin to rise from the other side of the door. He soon finishes off and cleans up before walking back out to see the pair of them just stood there, not looking happy, waiting for him. Both sets of arms are crossed and Clare still appears to have a real problem with what she'd seen, or rather what she imagines she could have seen if she'd interrupted her friend.

~ ~ ~

That night there is a feeling of betrayal as the three of them walk home in silence. When they get back Jack walks straight in to one of the bedrooms and within seconds of getting undressed he is asleep.

TWENTY-SIX

The next morning Jack wakes and realises he is alone and immediately his mind recoils to what had happened the night before. He remembers meeting and liking Toby and Julie but then he also remembers the horror of the walk home. He rolls over in bed and silence is all he hears in the rest of the flat and for once that worries him. He wonders what kind of fall-out is going to be palpable between the three that day. His mood plunges in to ever decreasing pits of despair when he moves in to the living room and spots a lone figure asleep under a blanket. Whoever it is looks too good to disturb so Jack grabs his 'tobacco tin' off the coffee table and takes it back to the bedroom. On his way back he stops off in the kitchen for a glass of water. The hangover he was expecting has not materialised and he knows, from years of experience, that the best thing to do is drink water. Remain hydrated at all costs; which meant if you were going to smoke a joint as strong as the one Jack was about to you needed to drink lots of water.

Back in bed he downs about half-pint of water before even contemplating the rolling process. He goes for a simple single-skin joint packed with some of the finest Moroccan hashish known in the UK. He leaned back and sparked the joint, ensuring the ashtray was in the perfect position in case of any flares or hot-rocks falling. None did and he settled in to bed but again his mind flew back to the night before. Had Lisa really been in the bathroom with another man and if so who's to say they had done anything. It was then an image came to him that he would have difficulty shaking loose. The look on her face as Lisa stumbled out the bathroom and the fact she was struggling to pull her clothes back in to position. It was the look of a woman who had clearly been up to something. It soon became clear that another joint was needed, just to stifle the image of Lisa in the compromising position to the back of his mind.

After twenty minutes and with the image still dominating large in his mind and the second joint already smoked Jack knows he needs to watch something that will really keep him distracted. He is not in the right mood to read and he doesn't want to interrupt the sleeping beauty in the living room with music so he wanders in to the kitchen where he grabs his laptop.

He walks back to the bedroom and settles in for a morning of alone time. He clicks on the Internet browser and after a few minutes finds a site just right for him. There is a new girl on screen and Jack feels his cock grow hard. Aviva is dressed in a college uniform and is sitting alone in a lecture theatre with a professor. She is gorgeous, all glasses, big teeth and pert tits and as the film unfolds it becomes clear she wants to seduce him. The look of shock when finally his cock appears really turns Jack on, it is as if she has never seen one before and when she takes his cock in her mouth she can't help but gag as his full-blown hard-on fills her mouth. Shortly after he penetrates her tight pussy as she lets out a slight moan. Jack too lets out a moan as he can feel himself getting close to orgasm.

However no matter how turned on Jack gets he still can't shift the image of Lisa from the night before. Aviva and her lucky stud work through a whole host of positions as Jack manages to finally work his frustrations out but then just as he shoots his ejaculate in to a waiting tissue paper her face re-appears. She has the look of a woman who has just done something naughty and suddenly Aviva and Lisa are the same. They both look guilty but also pleasured beyond belief.

After cleaning himself up he rolls another joint before finally throwing his laptop on to the bed and making to get up. Standing, he fondles his bulls before pulling on a pair of clean boxers. He lights the joint as he looks around the room. He is alone and right now he feels more alone than at any time since he'd met Clare. He walks to the kitchen where he makes a big mug of tea whilst smoking on the joint. He is suddenly reminded of his single life when a lot of mornings where spent drinking tea, smoking joints and watching porn, in particular on Sundays like this.

Instead of disturbing the sleeping beauty in the living room he decides to sit in the kitchen smoking on his joint and drinking his mug of tea. However he still can't shift the look on Lisa's face as she stumbled out of the toilet from his mind. It looked like it was there to squat for a while longer and during the next half-hour he decides that maybe it is best to just smoke another joint and hope it destroys all memory of the previous evening. Eventually he decides to go out for a walk but as he goes to pull on his coat Clare walks out of the second bedroom.

"Morning," she greets him.

"Oh hiya, I was just going to pop out for some air. I'll stay though if you ..."

He was going to finish with 'want some company' but then spotted the anger that was still quite clear on her face.

"Ok, you going to be long? I'll get us some lunch if you want for when you get back?"

"Sure, that'd be nice love, thanks … I should be back in about an hour but no rush on the food, I could give you a hand if you wanted?"

"Hmm, maybe … we'll see. Could do me good today to keep my mind on something …"

At that point Jack took his coat off, knowing he wouldn't get the air he needed. He knew he would have to sit down with Clare and talk about what had happened at the party and the implications it had on their lives. Jack wasn't completely sure it would change anything besides the relationship between the two women but as one of these women had just caused him to upheaval his entire life he felt compelled to listen. He needed to know what was going to happen.

They sat in the kitchen, drinking tea as Clare told the tale of her relationship with Lisa. They had met at university but then Lisa had moved down here to escape an obsessive boyfriend and with the dream of becoming an artist. Clare began to cry as she told of losing her lesbian virginity to Lisa and how the pair had grown so close during the last eighteen months of university. Then it had changed with the move and they had grown distant until about six months ago when Clare received a message on a social networking site. Since then, Clare said, they had grown tighter than ever but now Clare felt betrayed. It turned out the person in the bathroom had been Julie.

Jack made no attempt to understand how but he could tell that Clare felt threatened. He rolled a strong joint for them to share and as he passed it to her he asked simply,

"Well, what are we going to do today?"

The look on her face suggested Clare was giving this some thought when there was a loud crash in the living room. Clare groaned, Jack felt confused and suddenly there was another loud crash. Jack accepted the joint back and smoked deeply on it, feeling himself finally getting that image from last night out of his mind. There was another loud crash and Clare stood up, heading off in the direction of all the commotion.

Suddenly what sounded like all hell broke loose in the living room and all he could hear were female voices shouting at each other. He finished the joint, moved over to the door, pulled on his coat and snuck out.

TWENTY-SEVEN

The late-morning sun poured in through the house-door as Jack opened it whilst trying to ignore the loud screaming sounds coming from their top-floor flat. It sounded like an explosive argument was in full-swing and Jack did briefly think of going back upstairs to see if there was anything he could do or say to help calm the situation. He then realised he had no idea what he could say to quell the situation so he went with his first idea; fresh air and plenty of it, visual stimulation that would keep his mind off Lisa's guilty look and a decent walk to help him forget everything.

He walked down towards the beach and stood, surveying the scene laid out before him, from the promenade. It was a beautiful sight indeed. Jack's eyes suddenly fixed on a woman, lying alone and towards the sea. She is wearing a tiny black bikini that leaves very little to the imagination and her body looks bronzed and well toned. She rolls over to reveal a pert yet firm bum that is barely contained by her bikini pants. Jack is mesmerized and can't take his eyes off her but she does nothing, just remains lying there. She seems to enjoy being the object of lustful looks. She rests her chin on her splayed hands and for the first time Jack can feel her eyes making contact with his. She then lets one of her hands out from under her chin and suddenly her top is undone. Jack feels his cock growing hard but does nothing about it. His eyes move

161

away from her to another equally beautiful woman; this one is wearing a sleeveless tight T-shirt and a pair of red bikini pants.

He can feel his cock getting harder and decides to move back to a seat. As he sits down he notices the topless bronzed goddess look up at him. She stands up and it feels like every set of male eyes move to take in her vision as she moves in to the surf. Jack looks at her playing around in the sea with her impressive breasts bouncing around in front of her. She keeps looking over towards him but Jack knows any further action would just lead to an increase in the tension back at the flat. What could he have done anyway, he'd promised to be back at the flat in an hour and a beauty like that would take hours, if not days, to satisfy.

When he realised there was nothing he could about it he stood up and began walking west. In the west lay Hove, boring, suburban Hove where no temptation lay. It only took him about fifteen minutes to realise that was a fallacy when he bumped in to Julie. Remembering what had happened last night and what Clare had recently told him he was unsure of how to act when she acknowledged him with a wave and moved in his direction to talk.

"Hiya," she beams, it seems completely unaware of the mess she has apparently caused back at the flat.

"Oh hey," Jack responds, hoping that will deflect her in to saying something, anything so he could get his mind together enough to know how to act.

"Did you enjoy yourself last night?" she responds.

Jack has no idea of how to respond to a question that is so loaded. He could vent him fury or he could come out with some civilized banality to hopefully distract her but as his mouth opens he is unsure what is going to come forth.

"Fancy a joint?" is all he can muster.

"Sure, you got a pre-rolled one or do we need to go somewhere quiet?"

"Somewhere quiet would be good" Jack responds.

~ ~ ~

With a quiet place located Jack begins to build a nice joint for two and finally Julie stops asking him questions. After fifteen minutes of silent contemplation Julie finally turns to Jack and tells him how she'd enjoyed meeting Clare and him the previous night.

"That Lisa, ain't she something?" she concludes.

Jack is unsure of how to reply; his mind is a fog of weed and he can only tug again on a long toke. He lies back after passing her the joint.

"I enjoyed myself too, Toby seems like a cool guy ..." was all he could muster. He hoped that would be enough to stop her talking.

"Well, it ain't going to be me and Toby for much longer ... I'm dumping him."

"Oh, why's that?"

"Just bored ..." she leans in and after inhaling deeply on the joint places her mouth against his and performs a blowback which sends Jack spiralling. He relaxes in to the grass before realising that her mouth is still on his, now in the process of kissing him.

Sliding on to his back he feels her climb on top of him and again he can feel his cock growing hard. She is wearing a tight T-shirt with a fleece over the top and a short skirt. He can feel her panty-covered crotch grind down on his groin and she begins to kiss him more passionately.

When Jack realises what is happening he sits up and pushes her off him.

"What you doing?" he asks annoyed at her actions.

"Well Jack, I like you ... I like you a lot."

"Yeah, so what. Do you know what you've already put me through this morning?"

Julie merely looks confused but Jack has finally lost his inhibitions and lets rip at the woman who, even though not present, had driven him from his lovely flat that morning.

"Well your actions last night may have cost me the best situation I've ever had. Get it now?"

Julie looks more confused than ever.

"Did you, or did you not fuck Lisa in the bathroom last night?"

"No, that wasn't Lisa ..."

"I saw Lisa stagger out looking dishevelled and pulling her clothes back in to place. Clare got really angry and I left the pair of them in the flat this morning arguing, in fact screaming at each other."

"Oh, but I fucked myself in the toilet last night. I was thinking of you, I was all alone bar a big dildo I'd taken for company ..."

"What, now you're just messing with my head," Jack concluded as he stood up and began to walk off.

"Hey, where you going?" her voice pleaded as her stoned mind finally worked out what was going on.

"Home, I'd rather deal with two screaming women than your ridiculous mind-games. Now leave me alone."

As he walked off he could feel her following him but he chose to just ignore her and hope she would grow bored before he got back to the flat. Fifteen minutes later and with Jack completely freaked out by all he had seen and done on his short little walk he just wanted some space. He stood on the green and looked out to sea. If he couldn't get space here, he thought, where could he? It was an impossible, nee ludicrous situation he felt himself in. Six months before he couldn't get a woman to look at him and now ... well, he was confused to say the least and it wasn't all down to how much weed he'd already smoked that morning. In the square all Jack could hear were the gentle waves of the sea lapping at the beach, the sound of car engines driving by but most loudly of all two female voices. Lisa and Clare were still clearly at war in their living-room and Jack, after he'd remembered the fruitless hunt for a 'local' pub the night before, decided his best option would be to continue his quest until somewhere had been found. It wouldn't matter how long it took he needed to find a place; somewhere to seek refuge, a place where maybe he could just slowly drink himself in to oblivion.

TWENTY-EIGHT

Jack turned and then walked beyond the corner where the flat was located, heading east towards the pier that dominated the off-shore scene before he noticed a little path leading in to town. Despite stopping for a few minutes of contemplation on the square Jack could still feel Julie's presence behind him but all he really cared about right now was finding a drink. And then after a few more he hoped he would be ready to go back to the flat or at least that's what he hoped. Stopping at the bottom of a street he'd never seen before he turned for the first time since leaving the square and noticed that Julie had, it seemed for now, lost his trail. Looking up the street Jack was pleased to see a couple of bars open. The first one seemed pretty good from the outside and Jack decided to walk in. Within seconds he knew it was the right move to make. A loud AC/DC song blared out a set of speakers and a young barmaid walked over to where Jack was sitting.

"Hi, can I get a pint of Heineken and a shot of dark rum," Jack stated, finally free to be left alone.

The music was loud enough to keep him distracted and the gorgeous young barmaid was enough for his eyes to remain distracted.

"Had a hard day?" the barmaid enquired as she poured Jack his first pint.

"You could say that, god what a mess it all is." Placing the pint in front of him he took it from here and gulped down a large amount as she poured him a dark rum.

Jack downed the rum and promptly ordered another. He was in the mood for a drink, an annihilation of the senses that would banish all the bad, or weird, shit that had happened to him. He drank down half of his beer and ordered a third rum when suddenly there she was; Julie. She had tracked him down and as soon as she walked in she noticed him and made a beeline straight towards him.

"Look, what are you doing?" Jack asked, pre-empting her with a biting remark from the off.

"Well ..." she seemed shocked that he was still angry.

"No, you look, just leave me alone. Don't you think you've done enough damage already even if you are innocent of any wrong-doing last night?"

"How did you work that out?"

"All I know is my girlfriend, a woman I uprooted my life to stay with, is pissed at me and her best mate because she thinks you or someone at your party fucked our friend last night."

"Well I promise it wasn't me ... I told you it was someone else ... I told you what I was doing ..." A tear appeared in the corner of her eye and Jack knew for the first time that she was telling the truth. Now, he thought, what should he do?

"Ok, so what now? What do you want?"

She sat down next to him and smiled whilst massaging his thigh through his jeans.

"No, I told you," he said, slapping her hand away, "I love Clare, I want me and her to work out this situation and whilst I trust you are telling the truth I don't believe you can have any involvement in an amicable reconciliation."

"Well, mind if I stay for a drink?"

"I'd rather you didn't but if you really want to ... well, I can hardly throw you out can I?"

She ordered a couple of beers and a silence feel between the pair as they continued to drink. Jack had never known a day like it, it seemed wherever he went women were there flaunting themselves in front of him. If only he had been single he would have plenty of opportunity but slowly his mind drifted back to Clare. That beautiful face, the wonderful body, the magnificently filthy yet intelligent mind; she was everything he had ever wanted and as he drained his third beer he got up, pulled on his jacket and told Julie he was going back to the flat. She asked if he wanted her phone number but he resisted and told her they'd chat some other way. He hoped that situation would never transpire but somehow he knew that he hadn't heard the last of Julie.

As he walked out the door to the bar he made straight for the beach. It was much later than the time he'd told Clare to expect him and suddenly he felt nervous about what may face him upon arrival back at the flat. As he walked down towards the beach he noticed it was now much quieter; he found somewhere quiet and proceeded to roll another joint. That would help him deal with whatever situation he encountered back at the flat. As he walked back along the beach towards home the joint smoked smoothly and succeeding in calming his mind and finally when he felt calm and composed enough to deal with anything. As he walked up to the house an eerie silence dominated the scene. The argument, it seemed, had stopped or maybe one of them had just gone out. He would only know once he was back indoors.

Walking in to the flat he was pleased to hear the quiet hum of the cooker whirring from the kitchen and a calm silence emanating from the living room. He walked in and after placing his jacket on the back of the door and kicking his shoes off he walked towards the living room.

Within seconds of walking in Jack was greeted by Clare throwing herself at him. She immediately began to cry.

"What is it? I'm sorry I'm late, what's happened?"

"She's gone ..."

"Who? Lisa? Where? Where has she gone?"

"I don't know," she said as the torrent of tears increased.

"Oh god, I'm sorry ... I knew I should have stayed but when I heard you both screaming at each other I thought you both needed some space."

"What? You heard us arguing and yet you still went for a walk, why do you smell of perfume and beer?"

"Well ..."

"Oh I can't believe it, are you cheating on me?"

"No of course not, I love you!" he retorted.

This placated her enough and she sat back down on the sofa, thankfully calming down before his very eyes. Jack walked in to the kitchen and checked the oven, it was empty and the smell was clearly from something that had been prepared and eaten earlier. He walked back in to the living room and sat next to Clare on the sofa before he began to roll a joint.

With the joint rolled and in the process of being smoked Jack finally got the nerve up to ask about the argument. It transpired that Lisa had admitted fucking someone in the bathroom at the party, a guy in fact, but she was just horny because of the pot and the booze. It hadn't meant anything but Clare didn't believe her and so the argument had ensued until the point when Lisa, annoyed at Clare's reluctance to believe the story, had stormed off. Clare began to cry again but this time Jack put his arm around her and pulled her tight.

"Don't worry I'm still here for you ..."

"Well, thank god for that," she responded snuggling her head deep in his chest. A peaceful silence feel between the two and Jack developed the routine of rolling a new joint as he passed the old one to Clare to finish. After a few like this Clare had enjoyed enough so Jack was forced to smoke alone. After the day he'd had he felt he needed a couple more to knock him out for sleep, it was after all a Sunday and he had that long commute to look forward to the next day. That night they slept together and that was all, sleep from eleven until six-thirty when Jack's alarm sounded and the new working week was upon them.

TWENTY-NINE

The alarm sounded and Jack struggled to get himself out of bed. Clare was lying next to him, looking radiant in her long T-shirt with her hair sprawled over the cushion. Jack would have loved to take her right there and then but after the weekend he felt unsure of how she would react and what's more he needed to get out of bed and get to work. A large breakfast of coffee, toast, cereal and the ubiquitous joint was needed.

The commute gave Jack a chance to think about what had happened at the weekend; was it the end of his new dream life or was it merely a blip, something the three of them would get over. Jack hoped it would work out this way that it could be resolved as he'd sacrificed so much for this chance and it had often felt like a last chance for happiness.

Work passed off easily that day with Jack battling through a mountain of photocopying for a whole barrage of meetings that were to take place that week. That night when he arrived home Clare was cooking up some pasta but there was still no sign of Lisa. They sat in silence as they ate their dinner, unsure of what to say or what was going to happen now that Lisa had appeared to have gone. Tuesday passed in a similar fashion but when Jack's alarm rang the next morning he was happy to see Lisa had returned and was asleep under a blanket in the far corner of the living room. He reasoned she had over-indulged over the last few days and needed some space so he just went through the routine of preparing for work. He knew that by the evening and his return the situation would be a lot clearer, he was sure that Lisa and Clare would sit and talk that day.

Work was a welcome distraction for once as he got to grips with updating some student records on the computer system in preparation for an annual governmental report. It was only when he walked out of work in fact that he realised what awaited him at home, or at least what he hoped for. He hoped that he would arrive back at the flat and Lisa and Clare would have made up and everything would be back to how it was in those first few glorious weeks of cohabitation. The fucking, the weed, the drinking, the companionship and the food, all of that would return and all of them would be happy again.

Arriving at the flat he was pleased to hear some music playing from out of the top floor and reasoned it was better than the sound of screaming or arguing people. Ascending the stairwell it became clear that the music was the Beach Boys and the smell of that Moroccan hashish suggested that everything was back to normal. Unlocking the door he was pleased to be greeted by Lisa on the other side, offering him a joint even before he'd taken his jacket off.

"I'm sorry Jack, I'm really sorry for all the hassle I caused over the weekend ..."

"No problem, is everything back to normal now? Is Clare here?"

"Yes, yes she is."

With this Jack took a large toke on the joint and

walked in to the living room. Lying on the sofa in a T-shirt and jeans outfit was Clare; she looked happier than she had at any time since the party. Jack took another lungful of smoke and offered her the joint.

"Now, how about some dinner? How about I rustle something up for the three of us?"

"What a hero you are lover," Clare said, visibly stoned and almost falling off the sofa.

Twenty minutes later and Jack had prepared a Mexican odyssey – fajitas with a fantastic hot veggie chilli and some tortilla chips. The three went to work on the food as Jack took occasional hits from a bottle of cheap Spanish wine he'd found in one of the kitchen cupboards.

With dinner done the three settled down to a night of weird sixties pop, cheap Spanish wine and the rest of Jack's hashish. That night the three of them slept together again but again that was all, nothing more than sleep.

At work on Thursday Jack received an email from Frank; it reminded Jack that it was his birthday in a couple of weeks, a big one indeed, the big 4-0. Middle-aged beckons so what better way to usher it in than by having a big party at his great new sea-front flat. Jack thought it might be a good idea but he knew he would need to talk to Clare and Lisa first, the scars from their last party were still pretty raw but the healing process had at last began. That night he bounced through the flat's front door full of joy with the idea that perhaps his infectious enthusiasm would be so over-whelming they couldn't possibly say no.

"Evening all, how is everyone?" he beamed upon gatecrashing the kitchen.

"It's all good," Clare responded, " ...you seem perkier than normal this evening..."

"Well I got an email today, it reminded me of a major upcoming land-mark" he announced.

"Oh yes, what would that be then?" Lisa asked.

"Well, it's my fortieth birthday next week ... fancy us having a little soirée Saturday week?"

"Yes, we could make it a flat-warmer too if you want?" Lisa suggested.

"Cool," Clare and Jack echoed in unison. It seemed as if things had returned to normal a lot quicker than maybe Jack had hoped or expected.

~ ~ ~

After dinner the three settled down in the living room to watch a couple of cult movie classics, *Driller Killer* followed by *Faster Pussycat Kill! Kill!* They had long been a couple of Jack's favourite movies but even now, after watching both a lot of times, Jack needed one last joint before he got to finally retire to bed. That night was like one of the first ones they'd spent together; they'd smoked a forest of weed, watched some cool movies and then, finally, after almost a week, made love in a wild, unrestrained exhibition of unadulterated lust. It was some night. The next morning Jack's alarm went off and, after dragging himself from his bed, he went through his before-work ritual; a strong mug of coffee, a joint and a decent round of toast and cereal. As the long commute began Jack feared work would be a real long slow drag but fortunately it flew by. Jack was pleased when Kerry accepted his invitation to the party; he knew with her there it wouldn't get out of hand as she, on their nights out, often proved to be the rock around which Jack's occasionally wayward self sailed, clinging to her as a focus of sanity and reality.

CHAPTER THIRTY

The weekend passed in a haze of weed smoke and much too quickly Monday morning reared its ugly head in to view. The three of them didn't really mind, it had been a pretty stressful few days after last weekend's party and after the bout of insane fucking on Thursday night they all needed a good rest. What's more it was going to be Jack's birthday on Wednesday and there was still the big flat-warmer-slash-birthday party the following weekend. The party was shaping up nicely; all the people who Jack wanted to attend had confirmed their invitation and they'd arranged to meet at various times throughout the day at the one pub in the North Laine they all knew how to get too; the one with the mural of dead rock stars on the outside wall.

On the morning of his birthday, which Jack was pleased to have had the good foresight to book off work, he was awoken by a glorious sensation. Clare in that Britney outfit and Lisa just dressed in the sexiest underwear he'd ever seen on her; a very sexy black bra, garter belt and fishnet stockings with a tiny little G-string to finish off the outfit. They both looked good enough to go all day and as Clare went down on his already stiff cock Jack was in heaven; what a way to be woken up on your fortieth birthday, he thought as Lisa worked off Clare's panties and began salivating over her pussy and clitoris. It wasn't long before Jack was fucking Lisa in her deep, wet pussy as she sucked on a strap-on that had miraculously appeared from somewhere and was now attached to Clare. It sure was some scene and the three of them continued like that for most of the morning. Just in time for lunch the three of them collapsed, naked, on to the bed; completely worn out they seized the moment for a brief siesta. It wasn't until late in the afternoon that they actually made it in to the living room where Jack decided to roll a joint. Clare and Lisa had changed in to more normal clothes by now and they slumped on the sofa, all three of them squeezing on to the two-seater. For the remainder of the afternoon they sat around watching a movie, the weirdo-classic *Blue Velvet*. That evening, after a spot of really nice dinner, they went out to the bar Jack had discovered on Sunday afternoon. Fortunately it was different bar-staff so there was no one there he knew or who could drop him in to a new world of shit by telling all about his liaison with Julie. Whilst the three of them were having a fun night out two of them were clearly thinking about the possible repercussions of what a really big night would have on their ability to make it to work the next day; Jack knew there was no way he could call in legitimately sick the day after his birthday. Everyone would know what had really happened and he would be in real trouble, something he couldn't ever afford. Not now, not at this stage when it was all so damn weird. He needed the security of the job, how else could he afford the rent on the flat or his recreational routines? He didn't want to know so for once decided to act like a sensible grown-up. Maybe turning forty would change him more than he had thought it would. On the big night they were home by midnight and Jack went to bed immediately after smoking a strong joint and when his alarm went off at seven, he'd allowed himself a brief little lay-in, his head was fine and he went through his early morning ritual. The commute was fine that morning and Jack actually had the time to get himself a really fantastic coffee from a nearby shop on his way in to the office. That evening however was an entirely different matter, a train heading to Brighton had been intercepted by a UFO and all its passengers had been taken aboard. This caused a major head-ache for the rail authorities as there was an empty train stuck on one of the busiest lines in the south of England and the back-log soon built up to epidemic proportions, unfortunately the train Jack was on was one of those caught up in the mess and he didn't get through his flat-door until just before ten. As he was getting home Lisa was off to work at the gentlemen's club and Clare was working on some admin that she'd let slide at her job. Jack was so exhausted from his long day but he still needed that final ubiquitous joint before being able to even contemplate sleep.

Friday was a much simpler ride and Jack was pleased to enjoy a day that practically went to routine. Kerry confirmed her plans for attending the big party and they arranged to meet at around six p.m. in the pub before going to the house. There was no drink after work that evening as the pair of them guessed they'd enjoy plenty of chances to chat and drink the following evening. Kerry was coming alone and Jack knew it would be up to him to keep her in good spirits and company for most of the night. He hoped that his guests would help.

THIRTY-ONE

Jack woke early on the big day and treated the three of them to a lovely veggie fry-up for breakfast helped down with a few mug-fulls of coffee. It was a good way to start the day and would set them up for nicely for what was shaping up to be a bit of a marathon. Around twelve Clare announced that she had to go to work for a bit as she had the task of interviewing a new volunteer, so Jack concluded now would be the best time to set out to the pub; it would indeed be a long day from this point.

Jack was in the bathroom preparing himself for the day ahead when Clare left and suddenly he felt Lisa appear in the doorway. He had just climbed out the shower and the look in her eyes made it clear what she wanted.

"It's been a while since we had some fun alone, hasn't it?"

"Well ..."

He was cut off as she moved in close and kissed him, stifling his voice in the most passionate of ways.

'What the hell,' he thought as he helped her out of her T-shirt to reveal a bra-less torso before propping her up on top of the toilet cistern. Within seconds her panties were off and he was licking and drawling all over her pussy. She was going wild and as she was approaching orgasm he pulled her off the toilet and they began writhing on the floor fucking like wild animals. They both reach orgasm roughly at the same time and she pulled him close and kissed him again.

"Thanks lover," she said getting up off the floor and pulling her clothes back in to place. She had the same look on her face as she had at the party a couple of weeks previously and suddenly Jack felt as if he had done something terribly wrong.

"I better get out, my friends should be arriving soon and I don't want them thinking they've come all this way to wait for me in a pub. Having said that, you fancy coming with?"

"Sure, I've never met any of your London friends have I? It'll be a nice way to spend the afternoon ... maybe we could tell Clare and she could come after work?"

"Sounds like a plan," Jack agreed and ten minutes later Jack and Lisa walked out the house in the often-trekked direction of the train station.

They walked in silence but significantly, for Jack's mind anyway, she had her arm tucked in and her head rested on his shoulder. Walking along the seafront towards West Street they would turn and walk up the hill, surveying the debris of Friday night still strewn all over the pavement; left by those who came to visit, get drunk and probably either try and get laid or have a fight. The street hardly ever looked this bad but the bin-men were on strike, all Jack could think was good luck and thank goodness it's now October and not the height of summer or the smell of rotting kebab meat would be really unbearable. He decided it would be a good idea to take his friends another way on the journey back to the flat.

As they arrived at the pub Lisa went to sit at a table in the corner, an empty one that was quite large with maybe enough space to fit ten people. It was a little after one and

Jack ordered a pint of lager for himself and a gin and tonic for Lisa.

They sat down and almost within minutes Frank and a group of old friends had arrived. Jack was pleased to see that Frank had invited all the right people and the serious business of drinking began. By five p.m. Jack was feeling a bit giddy, he'd drank five pints and a few rum chasers and with Millwall winning and climbing the table, to the stratospheric heights of nineteenth, the day couldn't have been going better. Soon after another rum Kerry arrived and after one final round Jack knew the time was right to show them the flat. To show off his new life to all his friends who'd probably grown bored of his stories over the last few months. Jack knew that Frank was already jealous as he'd spent most of the afternoon desperately trying to chat up Lisa but she had just toyed with him. Whenever he thought he had a chance though she merely clutched Jack's arm again and with the suggestion of a whisper in his ear Frank was shot down once more.

After leaving the pub Jack and Lisa lead the group back through the narrow alleyways that dominated this part of town and towards the flat. As they came out on to a major street Jack's phone began ringing; it was a call from Clare. She was just leaving work and was desperate for a drink.

"Could we meet somewhere?" she asked.

Jack bought her up-to-date with what was going on and they agreed to meet at a spot near the flat where there was a take-away and an off-licence. After collecting supplies for the evening the group of friend's walked in to the top of the square. Jack simply turned to Frank and pointed up at the flat.

"That's our place there," he announced. The sound of jaws dropping all around was almost deafening. He heard a few notable 'wows' before Frank grabbed him from behind by the shoulders and shock him.

"You lucky bastard, you really have got it made ain't ya?"

"Some of us just get these lucky breaks," Jack replied, without even looking back, Clare now hanging off his arm.

When they arrived back at the flat Jack grabbed a few plates from the kitchen cabinet and asked if anyone needed some food. A few people agreed it would be a good idea after a day of drinking and Jack retired to the kitchen where he threw some food on a number of plates, grabbed a beer and walked back in to the living room.

"There's some food on the table in the kitchen if anyone wants any" he offered taking up his usual seat. Dinner was taken care of and the booze was being guzzled enthusiastically. The party was shaping up well and it was about eight when their door buzzer rang. Lisa got up to answer it as Jack passed a joint to one of his London friends, Amy, who he'd fancied for years. He was glad that Frank had persuaded her to come, why he wasn't sure but it felt good to have her around.

Moments later Jack's mood was deflated when Julie and Toby came in to view; whilst he liked Toby on first impression he was still unsure of how to act around Julie, particularly after last week's little rendezvous. Fortunately he managed to make sure that Clare got nowhere near Julie unless he was nearby; fully able to hear and possibly take action on anything that was said that could lead to negative repercussions. Despite this worry the party was going well, his London friends were mingling well with the Brighton people and even amongst themselves. It wasn't a wild night yet but it was shaping up nicely in particularly when factoring in the amount of pot and booze the Brightonians had bought with them. It appeared that Kerry was ingratiating herself with the Brighton group and Jack could tell by the glint in her eye that she was enjoying the weed that was being passed around. By ten Jack had only had to roll one as there was always something being passed to him, which he would invariably and gratefully smoke before passing on, not needing another hit until the next was passed to him.

The night grew wilder the later it got, the more drink consumed and the more joints were smoked; the music grew more raucous and louder and by midnight The Sonics were blasting out of Jack's dilapidated record player with their classic song *Strychnine*. It was getting pretty wild and a lot of people had seemed to split off in to various couplings. Jack was pleased to see Frank getting on particularly well with a new friend of Lisa's, a young sexy woman named Trudy who she'd met whilst working at the gentlemen's club. Jack was enjoying the scene and the party was rapidly becoming the best he'd ever been too; that was saying something considering his wild days of youthful exuberance.

Around two a few of the couples had gone off to their respective homes and the party was now down to only the really hardcore partiers. Much to Jack's surprise Frank and Trudy had taken a room, the would-be art studio, and it was clear what they had in store for each other. Kerry had asked to stay and once the last of the Brighton crowd left just before three she made her way to the second bedroom. It was going to be some night yet despite the fact that the three of them, Lisa, Clare and Jack, were now alone.

The two ladies, after letting the final party-goers out of the flat, walked over to Jack and asked him simultaneously, in that eerie way that twins often do, if he would like to open his present now. He instantly knew what they meant and a broad smile spread across his face. Lisa leaned in and kissed Clare passionately whilst also helping her out of her T-shirt; Jack sat back and took in the show that was unfolding before him. It was going to be some night …

Clare moved to undo Lisa's shirt and reveals a naked torso beneath and those magnificently pert breasts.

"You like this, don't you? You're such a dirty old man I don't know what we should do to you" Clare teased walking over to him letting her mini-skirt falling to the ground.

"I do you filthy whore, I fucking love it!" Jack purred knowing Clare loved it when he talked dirty to her. Clare pulled a pair of handcuffs from somewhere and quickly chained Jack's hands behind his back.

"Well you naughty boy we are going to get you so turned on you're going to want to explode." He sat back resting against his restrained hands and watching the scene unfold; Clare started rubbing her over Lisa's stomach and breasts before moving over towards him and began grinding her tight bum into his crutch. This was sending him over the edge as he became increasingly turned on, particularly when he became aware of Lisa playing with his girlfriend's nipples whilst kissing down over her stomach. Lisa began kissing around the outline of Clare's hot black panties whilst noting that Jack's massive erection was now clearly visible through his jeans.

"Well, look at what we have here!" she teasingly pointed out to Clare.

"Ohh, it does look like we got the old boy excited... what do you reckon we can do with him?"

"I know what he'd like," Lisa announced pulling her friend close and helping her to the floor. Within minutes they were both naked and in a 69 position, pleasuring each other with wild abandon. Jack couldn't take his eyes off the scene but was beginning to feel incredibly frustrated at his lack of involvement.

Looking away for the briefest of seconds Jack noticed his friend and work colleague Kerry stood in the doorway to the second bedroom looking out into the living area whilst taking in the view. It was clear that Kerry had witnessed the whole scene and was enjoying it. She spotted Jack staring at her and immediately became worried about how he would react to seeing her becoming aroused over the scene. Jack didn't mind, he had always knew Kerry was a little on the kinky side and he would not have been surprised to find her enjoying the show. He smiled and mouthed 'it's OK' in her direction. If anything it turned him on even more knowing that she was watching them all.

Clare looked up at her lover, still chained to the chair, and realised that whilst he was very turned on he was not really enjoying this experience, his frustration was becoming palpable. She sensed that he would enjoy it a lot more if he was free to join in so she pulled herself away from Lisa, who was writhing in delight on the living room floor with her pussy in full view of anyone wanting to watch. Clare undid the handcuffs whilst Lisa simultaneously unbuckled and removed his jeans for him. It was not long before she had his full seven-inches in her mouth as Clare licked her out whilst fingering her now wet pussy. When he was not keeping an eye on what the girls were doing he would look over towards Kerry to ensure she was still watching. Lisa was still sucking on his dick and Jack sensed that he was getting close to a mind-boggling huge orgasm. He pulled her face to look at him and she immediately knew what he wanted; he pushed Clare off Lisa and ploughed his rock-hard dick deep in to Lisa's pussy. It was only a matter of seconds before he came loud and hard; a mind-blowing orgasm that left him feeling nearly delirious.

Kerry looked on aghast at seeing her friend act with such confidence in such a situation and it was clear she was turned on and was playing with herself from behind the door.

Jack pulled Clare close and kissed her with all his passion as she helped him out of his last piece of clothing, his T-shirt was thrown over towards a pile of clothing in the corner of the room.

"Hey," Jack said, teasingly pulling Lisa towards him again, "looks like we got someone who's enjoyed our little show." He directed his view towards Kerry and Lisa knew what she needed to do next.

Moving away from Clare and Jack she walked over to

the bedroom where Kerry stood dumbstruck, unsure of how to act.

"Well, look at what I got here; you feeling a little nervous about what to do? No problem, I'll show you everything. Anything you want ..."

The pair passed out of sight and in to the bedroom but the sounds of passion were soon emanating from the room as it became clear what was going on behind the door. Jack and Clare moved off to the master bedroom and spent the next few hours pleasuring each other bringing to an end a night Jack had looked forward to and that had actually exceeded all desires and hopes.

THIRTY-TWO

When Jack finally woke the next morning it became immediately apparent to him that he was alone and for the first time since he'd met Clare this felt strange, unusual. He'd somehow forgotten a lifetime of waking alone and wondered what had happened to his lover. Pulling on his T-shirt from the night before he moved to the chest of draws that housed all of his clothes, he reached in for a clean pair of boxers and as he walked to the kitchen he struggled in his generally awkward manner to get them over his moving legs. The kitchen was empty so Jack merely reverted to his morning ritual, he put the kettle on to make some coffee before moving in to the living room where he pulled the curtains open and after making up his coffee he proceeded to roll a joint.

Finally taking up his seat he took a sip from his mug before sparking the joint to life. He sat back and relaxed and took in the view out of the window. When he was alone he loved nothing better than this but he was soon distracted by a series of noises emanating from the second bedroom. He finished the joint and struggled to get to his feet; he decided he should go see how all the party guests had slept and what the state of play was. The third bedroom was empty, Frank and Trudy it appeared had found somewhere else to go to enjoy themselves, or more likely Jack thought, Frank had messed up and in the dead of the night had escaped the situation which Jack knew would have made him feel awkward. What lay behind the second bedroom door was a whole different matter; as he peered round the door he was astonished by what he witnessed. His girlfriend was handcuffed, just like he had been the night before, but this time to the bed. Kerry and Lisa seemed to be having all manner of fun with their tongues and fingers in his girlfriend's various holes. They all seemed to be enjoying themselves but it was still a shock. His girlfriend, his second woman and a work colleague all engrossed in coital bliss, it certainly turned him on but besides that he was unsure how to react. Suddenly Clare looked up and saw him standing in the doorway.

"Lover, come join us. I need you ..." she pleaded before Kerry and Lisa turned their heads towards him. They kissed passionately before Lisa stood and moved towards him, she was naked and Jack could feel his dick growing hard in his boxers.

"Ah, not right now ladies, I need to finish this," he said lifting his mug of coffee in to view, "and I still feel a little groggy after last night. How much did we drink and smoke!"

About thirty minutes later Clare walked out of the bedroom, clothed in just a pair of black panties and a T-shirt.

"How's your head, feeling any more human?" she asked as she moved through to the kitchen.

Jack took a huge toke on the second joint of the day and simply mumbled to himself. He felt a whole lot worse now than he had when he'd woken up but he tried to put on a cool exterior. It was hard waking up without her and to then see her being tied up by two other women, one of whom he worked with, was a hard thing for him to get his head round. Clare returned with her own mug of coffee.

"Do we need a re-fill honey?" she asked walking towards him.

"Oh yes please" he replied, thankful that she seemed to have dealt with all the over-indulgence a whole lot better than he had. She returned from the kitchen with another mug of coffee and placed it on the small desk by his chair. A silence feel between the two but it was a silence that suggested contentment rather than anything else. Jack finished his second joint and noticed it was approaching lunchtime. He decided he could maybe do with some fresh air; he would walk to the local newsagent and buy a paper and maybe some snacks, he knew he wasn't going to feel like cooking, to munch on that afternoon as the munchies were sure to hit at some point.

He took the scenic route down to the newsagent, adjacent to the now bare remnants of the destroyed West Pier, along the seafront. He had a feeling of utter contentment, a phcnomenon he was unused to, but something which, he figured, he would have to get used to. The fresh air was a blessing and Jack completed a circuit of the square from the other side before returning to the flat. On days like these, with a huge hangover polluting his soul, there was no better feeling than that of fresh air on his skin. It made him feel almost human again and by the time he returned to the flat he was feeling a whole lot more awake. Life as a forty-year old was turning out to be interesting but also fun and life-affirming. He could never had pictured himself in this situation six months earlier and it still sort of felt like a dream. Not only did he have one of the most beautiful women in town as his main girlfriend he also had a good friend who it was cool to mess about with occasionally, as well as a decent job and an amazing flat. After letting himself in to the block he began the trek up the three flights of stairs and a smile appeared on his face. Upon opening the door to the flat he was pleased to hear the gentle patter of conversation filling the air and the smell of a new vat of coffee being brewed. Could things ever be this good again?

"Hi love", he heard from the living room as he managed to get through the door.

"Hi", he replied before entering the living room where Clare, Lisa and Kerry sat awaiting his arrival. He threw the paper onto the coffee table and helped himself out of his coat happy to see that they were all now fully clothed and drinking the fresh coffee he had smelt from the hallway. There was a fourth mug placed on his desk by the seat he generally occupied. He moved over, sat down, took a sip, threw the sections of the newspaper he didn't want on to the desk and after rolling a roll-up he immersed himself in the sports section. After about twenty minutes he put the paper back on the desk and turned to the group. They were all sat around and reading the other various sections that Sunday papers are generally comprised of and Jack simply asked how everyone was.

"Well I feel a mess," Kerry replied, "the next time you invite me down remind me to bring an over-night bag with some new undies and a big jar of headache tablets."

Jack sat there; glad that his friend from work could look at the rather uncomfortable scene with a grace and humour that he could not have raised himself. Clare stood up and walked over to Jack; she sat in his lap and began to kiss him and he could already feel himself becoming aroused.

"Fancy some fun?" she asked. Her eyes glinted with a madness of a woman possessed by lust.

Lisa and Kerry began kissing and within seconds Lisa was topless as Kerry began nibbling on her nipples. The afternoon was shaping up to be a surreal and wonderful experience and within twenty minutes the four of them were in the main bedroom. As Clare passed Jack a joint to smoke he looked down, inhaled deeply, and saw Kerry working his boxers off. He simply laid back and let the inevitable happen; he was so stoned again that it barely registered that this could be something he lived to regret. Several hours later and after pretty much every conceivable position and combination had been attempted he felt himself doze off to sleep. It had been some weekend he concluded before sleep took him in its warm embrace.

THIRTY-THREE

Jack woke the next morning with the deafening explosion of an alarm ringing from his side-table. It had been a fair while since he'd woke in such a frazzled and delirious state but after the weekend he had just enjoyed what else could he have expected. He struggled out of bed, pulled on a clean pair of boxers and a T-shirt, before walking in to the kitchen. It was then it all came back to him. Sat at the kitchen table was Kerry, wearing what appeared to be some of Lisa's smarter clothes, and looking every bit like his boss; at some point over the weekend he had forgotten that she was his boss. He reckoned it must have been that moment when she had taken his stiff dick in to her mouth and sucked with all her might. He took a seat and a massive slurp of coffee before looking up.

Kerry looked at him before asking what the plan of action was. It was just after quarter-past-seven and she was keen to know how long it would take to get to work.

"We should probably be looking at leaving in about half-hour, get to the station by about eight ..."

Clare bought a huge plate of toast, smothered in Jack's favourite raspberry jam, and laid it out on the table. Jack took a few slices before disappearing back to the bedroom to finish getting ready for work. He would have to forego the smoking the joint part of his routine that morning as his boss was here and whilst having some idea of Jack's lifestyle she had no idea it was as bad as needing to smoke one for breakfast. He finished eating his toast and prepared a roll-up to help finish his coffee off with. He returned to the kitchen about five minutes before they were due to leave and took the opportunity to smoke his roll-up and finish his coffee. He still felt quite close to death but he knew the fresh air would help improve his state. He hoped he would get a seat on the train and that maybe, just maybe, he could catch up on some much-needed sleep.

Jack lead the way out of the block and Kerry followed him on a little known shortcut round the back of the big shopping mall, Churchill Square, which left them by the Clock Tower with the train station in clear sight. The atmosphere between the two was strange. He'd never experienced this tenseness with Kerry before but something had definitely changed since Lisa and Clare had been introduced into the equation. The sight of the three of them playing together on Sunday morning had obviously had a huge impact on him and that was more recognisable now than ever before. Then, with his mind full of drugs and his body suffering from the effects of all that alcohol, he had been simply too out of it to be aware of any feelings that were growing inside him. They had walked in silence and as they got to the station Jack stubbed out his final roll-up. It was going to be a long journey; it was going to be a long day.

'Christ,' Jack thought, 'what's going to happen now. What if something develops out of this that is beyond my control ...'

The departure board indicated their train was on time

and due to leave in two minutes. They moved forward, with the baying mob, and climbed aboard their train. There was going to be nowhere to sit, not this morning, every seat had been taken by the time Kerry and Jack managed to manipulate their way on to the carriage.

"Is everything alright with us?" Kerry asked as the train pulled out of the station, next stop Gatwick.

"Of course, let's not talk about it here though," Jack replied stiffly.

The train moved swiftly through the Sussex countryside and towards the metropolis. By nine Jack and Kerry had arrived at Waterloo East station and before they had even got to the ticket barrier Kerry's questioning had begun again. She wanted to know all about Lisa and more worryingly all about Jack's relationship with her.

"It's just been a bit of a weird weekend, hasn't it?" Kerry concluded as they began the walk across Waterloo Bridge with work in sight.

"You can say that again, it's been mental hasn't it? I don't think now is the time or the place for that talk though, do you?"

Silence feel between the two again and as they turned the corner on to the Strand Jack felt a sense of relief in the fact that he'd made it this far without having to answer any awkward questions from his boss.

~ ~ ~

Work passed slowly that morning but at least it was quiet and Jack was mainly asked to go make coffee. It seemed like a few people had enjoyed good weekends although Jack thought none had experienced anything quite like the one him and Kerry had. Around half-eleven though an email arrived from Kerry; it was a list of questions, some very personal, that she demanded immediate answers too.

The first question was the simplest of the lot but Jack knew if he answered it wrongly he would enter a world of shit.

'What is the situation between the three of you?' it asked him.

Jack thought momentarily before deciding that honesty would be his best policy. He replied that 'I'm in a relationship with Clare who in turn has a bit on the side, Lisa, who we occasionally share.' He didn't mention the few times when him and Lisa had been alone and fooling around; he just hoped that it was something not mentioned over the course of the weekend. He saw no reason why it should have and hoped for once that his instinctual reaction was correct.

'I really like Lisa, do you think she'd settle for a monogamous relationship with me?' was Kerry's second question. How was he meant to answer that he thought.

'That is something that only Lisa can answer' he replied after a brief think.

'Do you enjoy being with her? Does she enjoy being with you two?' was the third and final question. Again Jack was flummoxed about how he could answer such a question.

'I'm a man, I have needs and since I met Clare all my needs have been met. Lisa is just a tiny bit of that equation. Would you like me to stop involving Lisa?'

Lunchtime finally arrived and it wasn't long before Jack and Kerry were alone again. Kerry moved over to

Jack's desk and began throwing questions at him. He sat there, unsure of what to say or indeed the ramifications of anything he did say so decided his best form of defence would be attack.

"What's the situation between you and Lisa?" he questioned, not really caring about the answer but glad that at last the attention was away from him.

"Well I just spent the best weekend of my life with a woman I didn't know forty-eight hours ago... my mind is a mess and I've no idea frankly. I do really like her though. How into Lisa is Clare?"

"In all honesty love, I've no idea. They used to work together at that club, I suppose you know that, and god knows what they get up to when I'm out at work but it ain't really been a subject we've discussed. We all really like each other."

"Well, just do me one favour, please don't involve Lisa until I get to talk to her, OK?"

"OK," Jack replied. 'Anything for a quiet life,' he thought knowing full well if Lisa offered herself to him there was no chance he was going to say no.

With Tina back from lunch Jack took his turn. It had been a long morning but he knew immediately what would sort him out. A few minutes later he walked in to the nearest pub, ordered a whisky, a small beer and some food. When he finished he wandered back to work with his mind empty and any sense of guilt buried under a showering of alcohol. The afternoon passed in a blur of insane filing and at half-five Jack returned to the office to say good night to all his colleagues. He was glad to be out in one piece, it had indeed been a long day. As he began the descent to the main entrance he could feel a presence behind him; he turned and realised it was Kerry.

"So, have you decided what you're going to say to Lisa and Clare tonight?" she demanded in a forthright manner. She said it in a manner as to suggest that, for the first time, she was his boss and she wasn't going to take any shit off him.

"Well, I was just planning on talking to Clare; it's her who is the most attached to our current situation so I'll see what she reckons and then if I need too, well then I'll talk to Lisa. Does that sound OK to you?" He hoped this would stop her from asking any more questions.

"No, no it doesn't. I want you to tell Lisa how I feel about her, about what an impact she's had on my life in such a short time. Frankly I don't care what your little bint wants; I just want Lisa and me to be together."

"Who exactly is this little bint?" Jack asked in a state of disbelief.

"You know exactly who I mean... that little whore who's just interested in fucking everything up. Fucking it all up for me, for Lisa and ultimately Jack, for you ... I mean, look at what's she done to us in the space of a weekend, she's going to ruin everything."

"Hey don't talk like that, not about Clare. I'll sort it all out I promise."

"Oh yeah and how are you going to do that? Are you going to dump that whore?"

Jack could not believe what he was hearing; the whole situation was escalating beyond anything he'd expected.

"Well?" she continued, demanding an answer.

"Look Kerry, you're a special friend of mine and I'd do

anything for you, anything but that ..."

"Typical, just sort it out. I want to be with her and I always get what I want ..."

Jack tore down the stairs at speed and raced out the front door, desperate for some nicotine to relief the stress he was feeling building inside his head.

The train journey home that night was a torrid experience; not being able to smoke meant his mind was forced to deal with all the stuff that had gone on with Kerry. He knew it was going to be an awkward evening and as the train pulled in to Brighton station he still had no idea of how he was going to raise the subject with Lisa and Clare.

THIRTY-FOUR

Walking through the station concourse Jack began rolling a much needed ream of nicotine; he had a lot to think about on his way home and a nice roll-up would help concentrate his mind. He knew it was going to be a strange evening and he hoped both Lisa and Clare would listen to him and understand how the situation from the weekend had affected his day at work. For the sake of all his relationships and ultimately himself, he knew the power that Kerry had over him, he hoped he could work out a plan of action. His friendship with Kerry had crossed the line between work colleague and friend a long time previous. Add in to this equation that moment on Sunday afternoon when she had taken his dick in her mouth and it was a unique predicament he found himself in. Walking in to the square he knew that honesty was going to be his best policy; if he faced up to everything that had happened it might be possible for it to all return to normal at the earliest chance.

He concluded that it was his relationship with Lisa that presented the real problem; Kerry had not seemed to have any problem being shared around the group but it was clear who she now wanted. Despite these feelings he still felt he had not done anything wrong, he had only enjoyed the freedom the relationship offered. He knew what he needed to do though and as he slipped his key in to the flat's front door he had it all worked out. He just wanted to be friends with Lisa and to have Clare as his girlfriend and most importantly, for the sake of him and Kerry as well, not share her with anyone. 'This would be the difficult bit,' he thought 'getting Clare and Lisa to stop what they seemed to enjoy doing with each other so much.'

Upon entering the flat though he was surprised to find himself alone so he simply decided to return to his old routine. He sat in his chair, turned on the TV and proceeded to roll a joint. It was nearly seven p.m. and even after smoking the joint Jack could not help but wonder where Clare and Lisa were.

After finishing the joint he decided to look around the flat for some kind of note that may offer some kind of explanation. He thought it curious that they had not simply texted him, letting him know what was going on.

'Maybe, Clare had to work late and Lisa had gone out somewhere having grown lonely as afternoon had become evening. Whichever, it was odd that neither had texted him' he concluded, unsure of where that left him. He decided to text Clare.

An hour had passed, another joint had been smoked, but still there had been no reply. Jack decided to hunt around the freezer hoping there would be something easy to cook. It was the happiest moment of his weird evening that he found a pizza buried deep towards the back. Twenty minutes later and he was devouring said pizza with glee, knowing after he could smoke another joint. It felt like an evening he was going to be left alone. It was the first time he'd got the opportunity to do this and so he decided to catch up on some time devoted exclusively to him. The deafening silence from his mobile phone continued as he began to flick through his huge stack of vinyl. He soon found the delightful Slanted & Enchanted by the great Pavement and proceeded to listen to side one whilst smoking a third, his biggest and strongest so far, joint. It was shaping up to be quite a pleasant evening but the later it got the more he began to worry where Lisa and Clare could have gone. His phone had remained silent so he'd decided to text Lisa too.

'Who knows, maybe Clare's phone has died and she's with Lisa wondering why they haven't heard from me?' he thought.

By the end of the second side of the record he still had no reply and he was beginning to get really worried. His worried mood lead to some intense questioning and soul searching, 'where is she?' he wondered, 'what's going on between us?' He had no answers and then suddenly visions of his last relationship and how that had ended popped in to his mind. The terrible manner in which it had crashed and burned and how after it he had never really been the same again, how his self-medicating had pushed him beyond the realm of normalcy to a place where it would be impossible to return from.

He remembered how horrible it all was; the night he stood outside her flat in one desperate last attempt at getting her back. The conversation that night had led him to have a breakdown on the street, crying in the rain as strangers rushed past trying to get home. He had hated being alone again; those long cold nights after she had thrown him out were his lowest point and it was a place he had vowed he would never return too. But this night was shaping up to be another of those low points as his mind began extrapolating a worst-case scenario that made him shiver with fear.

With his best friend Frank some sixty miles up the road he feared he would just spiral out of all control if things with Clare simply disintegrated. To compensate he rolled the biggest and strongest joint of the night to try and distract his mind from thinking the thoughts it currently was. His phone remained silent and that silence was killing him, pushing him slowly towards the edge of reason, a place he had hoped he would never have to visit again. As the smoke took hold he began wondering about bed; it had been an emotionally draining day and for the first time in six months he had something to worry about. It was a large worry; he was living in a flat he couldn't afford by himself in a town where the only people he knew were either mad, bad or just really not his kind and his job was at the mercy of a love-struck woman. It was a nightmare situation but as he finished off the final joint he felt his mind finally relax. He knew bed beckoned, bed had always been his favourite place even before he'd met Clare. As the clock drifted round to eleven-thirty Jack felt himself begin to doze off.

THIRTY-FIVE

His sleep was soon to be interrupted as at around three a.m. Clare and Lisa finally returned; crashing through the flat's front door laughing hysterically at something. He immediately knew his sleep was over as his mind raced at a hundred thoughts a second.

"What now?" he heard himself say to no one in particular just as the bedroom door swung open. Stood before him was Clare looking gorgeous but sounding drunk.

"Baby, I want a smoke, can you make me one? Please, lover ..."

"Sure but why you so late?" he retorted.

"Oh I didn't finish work until late and decided I needed a drink so went to see Lisa at the club. That's where we met, well ..."

"You bought guests back?"

"Yeah, Lisa's been working this crowd for a few hours now and she's made a fortune! At least three months rent for all of us. Isn't that great?" she slurred.

Jack got his weary body out of bed and pulled on a pair of boxer shorts and T-shirt and followed Clare in to the living room.

"Could you make me a coffee babe whilst I roll you a big fat joint?"

"Sounds like a fair trade," Clare responded disappearing off to the kitchen.

The living room was some scene. Around him sat five women dressed in power-suits, that looked as if they had just been taken straight from the cast of any eighties US drama, and then there was Lisa. She was gyrating in front of the group, her skirt lay on the floor and she was playing with those fantastically pert breasts through her T-shirt. She was apparently bra-less and Jack could feel himself growing excited again.

He sat back and began rolling a joint strong enough to knock them all out when suddenly Clare returned, mug of coffee in one hand along with a three-quarter full bottle of vodka that Jack assumed had been left over from the party. In her left hand she carried a tray of glasses. She handed Jack the mug and after pouring several large shots turned to their guests.

"Jack," she announced, "these are our new friends. Ingrid, Svetlana, Maria, Petra and that one with Lisa is Agnes. She's a film director ..."

Jack nodded his head to acknowledge their presence but didn't look up until the joint was finally constructed. Looking up Jack saw Lisa writhing in front of Agnes who was becoming visibly turned-on.

"You'd be perfect Lisa, just perfect ..."

"You see Jack, Agnes makes films of an adult nature and she wants Lisa to fly to Moscow to star in an adaptation of Close Encounters she's working on. What's it called Agnes?"

"It translates in English to Close Encounters of a Horny Kind ... it's going to be my epic, my master-piece ... Lisa would be just perfect for the lead."

Clare passed out the shots to the four other women

who he slowly learnt had been used to make a film in London called 'Midnight in Soho'. They had played sex workers who stalked the streets of Soho looking for action, looking for the next customer. Upon finishing the construction job Jack took a large slug of coffee and felt it invigorate him sufficiently to light the joint. After a few hefty tokes he passed the joint to Clare who casually relaxed against his chest, she smoked the joint down to the end and Jack took this as his cue to roll another. Lisa and Agnes had in the intervening time disappeared off to one of the bedrooms whilst the four actresses sat and drank their vodka. Jack took a couple of hits before standing up and going off back to bed leaving Clare alone with the four strangers.

The next morning he again woke alone and he promptly dressed for work, he had no idea what the scene in the living room would be so he thought it best to be prepared for any circumstance. Walking through to the kitchen he saw Clare still holding court with the four visitors who were still listening intently to whatever it was she was saying. He made more coffee and some toast before realising that one of the women had come in to the kitchen. She stood in the doorway with her arm draped up against the frame. She was wearing a dark blue suit but before Jack could say anything she had removed her jacket and was walking towards him.

"We heard all about you last night ..." she said as she approached. She unzipped her skirt and let it fall to the floor.

"Now I want my turn ..." Jack looked at her; she

definitely had the body of a porn-star, huge yet seemingly real breasts, a tight stomach and a beautiful pert bum that just screamed for attention. She leaned in and kissed him and he did nothing. She kissed his lips, then his neck and slowly began to work her way down after lifting his T-shirt up. He felt himself grow hard in his boxer shorts and knew it was going to be a real task to get to work that day. Within ten minutes she had his dick inside her mouth and soon after they retired to the bedroom where they spent most of the remaining morning fucking in every kind of position. He knew his excuse for work the next day would have to be a really good one but he had no idea where to start. He'd already used too many weird alien/UFO stories for one person, maybe it would have to be a simple old-fashioned twenty-four hour virus.

By late afternoon Jack, Clare and their new Russian friend had pushed the bounds of decency to a new low and after a few hours of mutual fun they collapsed in a heap on the massive master bed. By late evening Jack had fully exhausted himself to the point where sleep came easily.

THIRTY-SIX

Wednesday came abruptly to Jack as his alarm sounded at seven and for the first time that week he felt rested enough to contemplate the thought of work. Work where Kerry awaited him; what would he say to her, he had no idea. He rolled over and saw Clare and their new friend entwined next to him. He leant over and kissed Clare on the nape of her neck before getting himself out of bed. After dressing he walked in to the kitchen where he found Lisa and Agnes. He knew he needed to talk to Lisa but now was not the time or place for that. She told him to sit down as she bought him over a big mug of coffee. There was bread in the toaster and everything seemed good. It appeared the other three women had left, Jack assumed they had gone back to some hotel they were staying at and as he guzzled down his coffee he didn't ask.

At half-seven he found himself ready so he set off for work. He knew he was going to be facing up to a whole load of shit at work so he thought it would be best if he got his head down and got some done before the others arrived. The commute that morning went like a dream; he was walking across Waterloo Bridge at eight-thirty and would be at his desk before nine, a full half-hour before most of his colleagues.

The first thing he decided to do was email Kerry. The message was simple but represented all that he wanted to say.

'Hi love, I hope we are OK and you've recovered from the weekend. I thought I would write today to say that Monday night Lisa and Clare were still at work when I got home. They didn't return until yesterday afternoon. I've no idea where they were, I was in the depths of my twenty-four hour virus and didn't want to ask. So therefore I didn't get a chance to talk to them about our situation, our problem. I just wanted to let you know that now I'm feeling better I will discuss it with them at the next available opportunity which should hopefully be tonight. I hope this is OK and can I ask that we don't discuss it whilst at work. I really hope our friendship is still rock solid and that we will eventually return to normal service.'

As his various bosses arrived at work Jack made a point to talk to each of them, to say sorry for his absence the day before. They seemed to believe him and nothing was said about it so Jack simply got on with his work. He worked hard for a couple of hours, he had a fair bit of work to catch up on, before deciding it was time for a break for a smoke and a fresh batch of coffee. He asked the office if anyone else wanted one and as he walked off to the staff room he had instructions to make three, including his own. He returned with three mugs and after dumping two with his colleagues informed them he was going to smoke a roll-up.

Walking out the institute's front door he sparked the roll-up and leant against one of the columns that formed part of the entrance to the grand old building he worked in. As he took the first big lungful of smoke he noticed Kerry walking out to join him. She did not look happy.

'Oh shit,' he thought knowing that what was to come wouldn't be anything to please him.

"I think there are still some things we need to talk about Jack," she said by way of introduction.

"OK, but I told you I'm going to deal with it tonight."

"Right, but there is a question I need an answer too. Yesterday you said she worked some place, well she only told me she was an artist. I want to know where she works."

"Well, I'll tell you she works at a, er … gentlemen's club. She's a dancer there but what she gets up too in that position I've no real idea as I've never been there."

"What? She's a dancer at a club? I must know more … does she fuck her customers? Is she a mad nymphomaniac?"

"I don't know I'm sorry …"

Kerry burst in to tears, all her pre-conceptions about those sort of clubs coming to the surface.

"Have you ever seen her with someone else?"

"No, never …" Jack lied hoping to diffuse the situation whilst finishing off his roll-up.

"Anyway, busy today, better get on. Lots of work to do …" he said before walking back through the door to the institute.

The afternoon passed with no further mention of the morning flare-up and again Jack was pleased to have made it through another day at work safe in his job and with the hope that the talk earlier had been a building block on which his friendship could be assembled.

After his commute back home he didn't rush back to the flat, he decided to go for a walk, to get some air and to have a think. His situation was better now than it had been a couple of nights earlier but there was still a foreboding of dread hanging over him. Walking past the club where Lisa worked he saw a big picture of her by the door, she was dancing provocatively with Clare and the picture left little to the imagination. He knew she would be working so decided it was best he didn't go in, he meandered through the rich part of town known as the Lanes towards the seafront. He walked along the promenade back towards the flat taking in the tacky sights that the tourists flocked to in their thousands to look at. The night was lit up by antique streetlights and Jack just wandered. He had no idea where he was going or what he was going to do when he got there but it felt good to be out, away from the stress that was obviously waiting for him back at the flat. In the distance Worthing was light up like a Christmas tree and Jack decided to sit down and smoke a roll-up. It was indeed a beautiful scene, the moon reflected off the sea and in the distance sail boats bobbed around. Jack relaxed and let his mind settle before deciding now would be a good time to go home and see what situation was waiting to confront him that night. Besides, he hadn't smoked a joint all day and it was now approaching nine p.m. and he was beginning to feel the need for a blast of narcotic delights.

Turning on to the square he fumbled for his keys in his jeans pocket and after slowly navigating his way up the stairs he slide the key in to the flat's front door. He was relieved to hear the sound of music, the beautiful Pet Sounds record by the Beach Boys, playing out from the living room and as he entered he asked Clare how she was.

"Yeah, I'm good thanks, a little confused after all that's happened this week but well ..."

"It sure has been an odd week, ain't it?" Jack concurred.

She stood up and moved over to greet him with a kiss and a hug.

"Have you eaten?" she asked.

"Not really, but my appetite isn't great today so think I'll be alright."

Jack moved over to the seat he always sat in and began his ritual of rolling a joint. The night passed off with little talk, merely the passing back and forth of several joints. That night they went to bed together at the same time and for the first time since they'd arrived in Brighton and the weird little set-up they dozed off to sleep together. When Jack woke the next morning he felt as if it had all been a weird surreal dream and that he was in fact back in London. It was only when he walked in to the living room and pulled the curtains open and saw the sea that he knew it had all been real.

Work was easy that day as Kerry had called in sick. Jack was glad of this and got a lot of work done free from the stress of having to worry about her wanting to talk. That was the last thing he wanted, to talk to anyone about that situation. He was glad to have a rest from the constant worry.

THIRTY-SEVEN

That evening, upon arriving back at the flat, he was pleased to again hear music playing in the living room. This time around it was the first Ramones album, at one point in Jack's life his favourite record as it was blasting through side two.

"Ah, the memories this brings back," he announced to no one in particular as he walked in.

"Hi Jack," Lisa said, "I think we need to talk don't you?"

His mood soured at the thought he now had to deal with the situation that had been plaguing his mind all week.

"It's your friend Kerry ..."

"Oh yeah what's up?" he retorted.

"Well, she seems a bit full-on. She keeps texting me, saying she wants to visit this weekend. I'm not sure what to say."

"Oh yeah, she's been trying to talk to me all week but today, fortunately, she called in sick."

"Oh god, I just wanted a bit of extra fun and she seemed like a cool older woman ..."

"Well yeah I thought she was a cool one too but after this week I can sympathise. Can you believe I've only had one cigarette break this week and she came running after me wanting to question me about you?"

"Oh no, so what have you told her?"

Jack began to tell her what he thought she wanted to know, about Kerry, about how he felt about the whole situation and what he thought she should do. Lisa sat back, seemingly relaxed, but then once Jack had finished talking she visibly exploded in front of him.

"Oh fucking great," she screamed, "so what you're saying is she knows everything and left plenty of space for her mind to extrapolate further ... shit!"

"No, it ain't like that at all," Jack begged, hoping to diffuse the situation that was unfolding.

"But you've told her about me and Clare, me and you, god forbid what else have you told her?"

"I promise I haven't told her anything she hadn't worked out already!" He was getting more flustered and concerned about what was developing out of their conversation. Clare stood up as voices became raised and went off to the kitchen; Jack hoped to get some dinner for them. His mind was bewildered about what to say or do and so he decided it was best to not say anything at all.

As an ugly silence began to fill the room Clare returned to announce that some dinner was now ready. Jack and Lisa followed her back in but Lisa simply grabbed a plate of food and disappeared off to one of the bedrooms.

Jack was exhausted, mentally and physically, and did not want to have any further arguments so decided to sit at the table in silence after thanking Clare for some nice food. Silence again filled the room. After dinner Jack went and sat in his chair and began his evening ritual, he turned on the TV, found something dumb and funny to watch whilst he rolled a joint. A couple of hours passed during which he remained mainly distracted before he'd reached a point of tiredness where he knew bed beckoned. Standing up he told Clare he was going to bed.

"Do you want to come join me?" he asked.

She looked at him and without even saying a word Jack knew he was going to be spending the night alone again.

~ ~ ~

The next morning, as he expected, he woke alone again. He felt a coldness to the flat that he'd never experienced before when he suddenly realised it was November. Winter was coming and it felt like it was going to be the coldest one he'd ever experienced. As he pulled the curtains in the living room it still looked like the middle of the night out of the window. The dark night perfectly reflected his mood once he noticed the sofa was empty which could only mean one thing in his mind; Clare had opted to spend the night with Lisa. Then it came back to him that Kerry would probably return to work that day and he would have to deal, again, with the whole drama of their lives. After breakfast and with his women still in bed Jack moved off to work. The journey was a nightmare as a series of possible scenarios with Kerry played out. By the time he got to work he was nearly hysterical with worry and this was compounded as he walked in to the building's grand entrance and saw Kerry stood, smoking a roll-up, seemingly waiting for him. As he approached the door he stuck out his roll-up and hoped she would say nothing.

"Jack ..." she intoned as he reached for the door.

"What?" he retorted, having no idea how else to deal with her.

"We need to talk ..."

"Not here we don't, how about lunch?"

"OK," came her somewhat meek response.

"Somewhere cheap, somewhere we can chat. I really want this whole mess sorted out, it's really doing my head in."

Giving her no time to respond he pushed the institute's front door open and began his way to the office. For the next few hours he worked hard, hoping to keep his mind distracted. One of his bosses always went for lunch early and as soon as she left Kerry stood and walked over to Jack's desk. All week he had been trying, with increasing desperation, to avoid this very situation but now it was too late.

"Have you had a chance to talk to Lisa?" she asked. It was supposed to be a simple question but Jack had no idea how to answer, what to say. He was exhausted with the situation and for the first time in months he just wanted to be sat in the pub with his old friends from his old life. He missed the certainty and routine of those times and as his head crashed in to his desk he began to cry. Not with physical pain but a mental pain that had been building to this climax ever since Lisa had first laid eyes on Kerry.

"Jack," Kerry sympathetically asked as she leant over him, rubbing the back of his head. His only response was yet more tears and Kerry moved over to her bag from which she pulled a bag of tissues. She placed an arm around him and offered him a tissue.

At lunch Kerry and Jack went to a local coffee shop and he filled her in on all that had happened, exaggerating some things to make her feel yet more sympathy for his predicament.

"I'll be completely honest with you," he lied from the

out-set, "I'm not sure what Lisa wants from you; last night she told me she enjoyed being with you but then she went to bed with Clare. I've no idea what's going on, not even with the woman who's my so-called girlfriend. We've hardly spent a night together since moving in and it's really doing my head in."

Kerry looked at Jack and sensed he was telling the truth and decided he was as responsible for this mess as she was herself.

"What we need to do is split Lisa and Clare up, then you can have your girlfriend back and I can hook up with Lisa."

"Sure, that sounds great but how we going to do that?"

"Well how about I come down and visit tomorrow, unannounced as such ..."

"Hmm, that could work," Jack agreed, through gritted teeth aware that this would completely freak Lisa out. First the texts and now an unannounced visit would be enough to scare her at the very least.

"Let me talk to her first, just to get a gist of where her minds at? Then I'll let you know, is that OK?"

"Sure Jack, you know this might even make our friendship even stronger ..."

Jack grimaced on the inside but on the outside a smile appeared across his face. He had never felt guilt like it, lying to one of his best friends about something that affected them both equally.

The afternoon flew past and suddenly Jack was aware it was a Friday night. He imagined his old set of friends arriving at The Bells to try and get the working week out of their system. Approaching the train station he momentarily thought of joining them but when he checked the departure board he saw a direct train to Brighton leaving shortly and so headed to the advertised platform. It was going to be a long weekend and where his mind would be at the end of it he was unsure, he didn't really want to think about it. The train passed through the London suburbs quickly that evening and was soon hurtling through countryside. Jack was sad that he couldn't see any of its picturesque scene as darkness had already fallen. The train had seemed remarkably empty that evening but Jack had just assumed that for the first time that week things were starting to go his way. It wasn't until he got home and switched to the news on the TV. It appeared a commuter train from Bedford to Brighton had been involved in an alien incident in the centre of London. All of the passengers had apparently been abducted somewhere between Blackfriars and London Bridge. Jack immediately knew that this was the train on which he had travelled, fortunately for him he hadn't boarded until after the incident at London Bridge.

After watching the news, agog at how close he had come to a close encounter, he sat back and rolled a joint. The news had frazzled his nerves and after the week he had lived through it was almost a final nail in the coffin. Again, he sat in his chair, alone. This time however he didn't care that either Lisa or Clare were there. He was pleased to have some time alone, some time to himself to just switch off from his life. He smoked one joint after another until finally he was stoned enough to not feel anything. At this stage of the evening Jack didn't care what happened and when Clare arrived home he simply waved at her and began preparing another joint, this time for them to share.

"Oh boy, it reeks in here Jack, how much have you smoked tonight?"

He didn't reply he simply handed Clare a joint to smoke. She gratefully took it off and sitting down took off her shoes and jacket and seemingly relaxed for the first time that day. It had evidently been a long week for both of them.

Clare smoked the joint until it was about halfway down when she sat up and offered it back to Jack.

"Thanks lover, but I think I'm doing OK here" came his stoned, slurred reply.

She responded by stubbing the joint out and moving off to one of the bedrooms. A few minutes passed before she came out in more casual attire.

"Hmm, you are looking sexy tonight baby ..." he slurred as she walked across the living room wearing a T-shirt and tight fitting jeans. She didn't say anything, she just sat down in the chair she'd occupied before, picked up the joint and sparked it back to life.

"How about I order us a pizza?" Jack offered, hoping if he was nice to her well she might reciprocate with some sexual favours.

"Sounds good how about a fishy one by way of a change?"

"Just what I was thinking," he concurred.

After finding a menu from a nearby take-away he sat back in his chair and picked up his phone. It was Friday night the young man told him down the other end of the phone line, it may take up to an hour before we can deliver. Jack said that was fine and after placing the order hung up and began rolling another joint.

"Where's Lisa tonight anyway?" he asked.

"Oh, didn't I tell you? She's gone to Russia to star in one of Agnes' new films. Isn't that great, she's going to make so much money we'll soon be able to lead a life of leisure!"

"What? She's gone to Russia! Wow, when did this happen?"

"Oh well it was planned last night, she flew out this morning. She'll be back by Monday though."

"Wow, I suppose one of the benefits of acting in porn is the lack of acting it really needs ... just do what comes naturally I suppose."

A couple of joints later and dinner finally arrived; Jack and Clare ploughed through the pizza in a matter of minutes, delirious with the munchies after a severe bout of narcotic indulgence. With dinner finished Jack moved over and sat next to Clare; he was feeling horny and it was obvious to Clare what he wanted.

"Not tonight lover, I'm on my period ... sorry!"

Jack was upset at the prospect of spending another night alone, another cold and lonely night in that big bed that was slowly becoming superfluous.

THIRTY-EIGHT

The following morning Jack was elated to roll over and discover Clare lying next to him; it had felt like an age since he'd last woken with her by his side and it felt good. He leant over and kissed her gently on the cheek. There was no response but still he climbed out of bed with a renewed swagger in his step. He walked off to the kitchen, got some breakfast for himself and continued his morning ritual with the first joint of the day. It was shaping up to be just another Saturday, almost akin to one of those he'd lived for years back in his previous life, back in London. The morning evaporated in a blur of weed smoke and still there was no sign of Clare waking as he recognised it approaching lunchtime. Eventually, about one p.m., she appeared. She looked just as beautiful as she had that first night they had met, how things had changed since then Jack thought.

"I've got to go in to the shop this afternoon, there is some stuff that needs doing and I've got to interview a bunch of new volunteers so you'll have the flat to yourself this afternoon ..."

"That's cool, it's Saturday so that means football, I'll keep myself occupied" he concluded.

"Great, I should be back about five or six, then we can have some dinner, fancy going out for a drink tonight?"

"Sure, some kind of normalcy would be good and you can't get more normal than going for a drink on a Saturday night can you?"

"Cool," she announced, shovelling down a slice of toast as she finished off her coffee, "I'll see you later then," she said before leaning in to kiss him on the cheek.

Jack, with a sandwich for lunch, walked back in to the living room and took up his position. The team news would be coming through in less than an hour and that gave him plenty of time to catch up on his social networks, his personal emails and the scores from earlier in the day.

After checking all that he began thinking of Lisa, he'd watched a lot of porn during his single days and knew that some of the Russian stuff was particularly hardcore. He wondered what kind of thing she had got herself involved in and before long his mind was tapping out keys on his laptop, searching for some clue as to what she was doing. He remembered the director's name was Agnes, he started there, and soon found a website that was devoted to her starlets. He recognised a couple of them from the night they had been at the flat and he particularly remembered Svetlana. She was a stunning woman of about six feet with long flowing blonde hair and a full bosom and firm bum. He clicked on her picture and suddenly a vicious scene where she was, seemingly, being forced to have sex with a whole gang of men. Jack's mind recoiled as the sight of this, he was an open-minded guy but this was even beyond his standards of decency. As he clicked back to the home page he scrolled down and there, all the way at the bottom, was a picture of Lisa. It stated that her name was Kristina but Jack knew it was definitely her. He clicked on her picture and much to his relief there was no film yet just a series of provocative pictures, which got Jack feeling turned on. At the bottom of the page however was news, really bad news. It stated that 'Kristina' was a new actress to the stable and her debut, entitled Gang-Bang Frenzy, was due to be uploaded in the next couple of days. Jack's mind ran through a whole load of scenarios that lead him to feel even more worried about his friend and what, ultimately, this could mean to Kerry. If she had freaked out at the idea of the 'woman she loved' being a dancer in a club how would she react to this new development.

Jack decided to roll another joint and go over to a football site, hoping to forget what he had just watched. The afternoon passed off peacefully, Millwall played out a dull, lethargic nil-nil draw that perfectly reflected his desired state of mind. With the game over Jack decided he would treat Clare to a true feast when she got back from work. Moving in to the kitchen he got some pasta from the cupboard and began preparations. Around half-five Clare returned home and Jack greeted her at the door.

"Dinner is almost ready my love, there is a joint waiting to be smoked in the living room ..."

She smiled, kissed him on the cheek and moved in to the living room. When Jack appeared in the living room carrying two trays, one covered with a variety of breads and the other their two main meals, he was pleased to see her smiling, sitting on the sofa with the joint three-quarters smoked. He laid the breads out on the coffee table in front of her and placed her plate on the now empty tray before passing it to her.

Dinner passed off smoothly and Jack was pleased to not have any questions to answer. After dinner finished he moved the plates and various bits of cutlery in to the kitchen. He would leave it to soak hoping it would be fine to leave until the following morning. Moving back in to the living room he sat down next to Clare and his arm slowly moved round her back to pull her in tight. For the first time in a long while things felt almost back to normal and Jack was glad about that. They spent the night making out like a couple of teenagers on the sofa, in between times smoking a series of joints. The idea of going out had dissipated with every passing joint and by eleven the pair of them had decided to give in to their desires and go to bed. It turned out to be one of the best nights since they'd moved south and by day-break Jack had barely had a moment's sleep, his sexual appetite, it transpired, had been insatiable. They fucked the night away until long in to the morning.

Sunday was a perfectly lazy day, typical of a normal Sunday for a normal couple. They even managed to make it out to the local pub where they spent most of the afternoon after eating a lovely roast lunch. It seemed that life was reverting to normality at last and Jack was happy for the first time since his party.

THIRTY-NINE

Monday morning came in to view with a bang. As soon as Jack got out of bed he knew something was wrong. Clare was lying next to him, sound asleep but he had a weird feeling that all was not normal. He leaned over and kissed her on the cheek before climbing from bed. After getting some clothes together he walked in to the living room and pulled the curtains opened. It was then he knew what the problem was; a huge UFO, in some circles it would have been referred to as the mothership, was hovering in the sky above the town. He looked up and it was all he could see. There was no sky, not today and he immediately rushed to his remote control, turning the TV on and clicking on to a news channel. His little town was all over the news. It was all bad. There was talk of an invasion and as he looked out on to the green bit of the square he saw what the news people were referring to as a welcoming party. They were waving banners and hands in the direction of the massive UFO but as yet no response had come from the ship. Jack didn't know what to do but he felt he should call work and explain that if he didn't make it in then it was probably due to what was happening. After leaving a message on his big bosses' answer-phone he remembered Clare.

"Clare," he said, shaking her awake, "wake up, you've got to come and see this. It's amazing what's happening out there today!"

She looked agitated as her heavy eyes slowly opened. "What is it? What could be so important you'd wake me at this unearthly hour?"

"That's it; something unearthly is happening, right now, right here ..."

A look of utter confusion came across her face but she decided, after yet more cajoling from Jack, to get out of bed, pull on some clothes and go see what all the fuss was all about. The second she walked in to the living room she stopped, dumbstruck at what she saw out of the window.

"What the fuck?" was her only response.

"It's amazing isn't it?"

There was no response this time, just totally bewilderment and confusion as to how to react to what she was seeing.

"What are we going to do Jack?" she asked, with a hint of worry and panic in her voice.

"I've no idea but I reckon we need to get out of town and like now, this thing, according to the news people on TV, they reckon it could be an invasion party!"

"Shit no, so how? How are we going to escape before they come for us?"

"Well I guess the train station is going to be chaos, how about a bus to the middle of nowhere?"

"Sounds like a plan," she concurred rushing in to the bedroom where she pulled on a pair of jeans and trainers. By the time she returned a real sense of fear and panic had taken a firm grip on her mental state; she had never thought that this would someday happen but here it was, a full-scale alien invasion. She couldn't quite believe it but she knew they had to get the hell out of town, possibly never to return again.

As Clare and Jack ran out on the street they took the least visible route to a bus stop Jack knew could help them out of their desperate situation. However when they arrived at the stop the message was clear; they were fucked. 'Due to unforeseen circumstances all services are suspended' the message stated rather obliquely.

"Shit, so what do we do now?"

Jack instinctively stuck him thumb out but after looking in both directions and not seeing a car in sight gave up on the idea of hitching a ride out of town.

"I don't know, shit, I really don't know. We've got to get out somehow."

Jack looked out at the sea where there was an armada of boats sailing off in to the distance.

"How about we go to the marina? We could maybe, hopefully, persuade someone to take us on board their boat?"

"Anything, yes ... just get me the fuck away from that!" she screamed whilst pointing up at the sky. Jack agreed and for the first time in years he began to run with Clare chasing behind but when they got to the marina the scene was bad. There were no boats left and there were hardly any people left with whom they could work out a way to escape. At that point Jack looked up at the sky and became pleased as slowly the mothership began to move off in a northerly direction, towards London. He looked at Clare and a sudden feeling of relief swept over them; they would be safe after all. As the mothership drifted off Clare deduced it was safe to go back in to town. She wanted to have a look around, to see if anything had happened that was out of the ordinary, as they both began walking back in to town it was clear plenty had happened. The town seemed deserted and those that were left seemed to be only capable of wandering around in a daze, spell-bound by what had happened.

Back at the flat Jack and Clare went immediately to the TV and tuned in to a twenty-four hour news channel. It was all bad news, there were ships abducting people all over the planet but the authorities were bemused as to why, why this was happening? It seemed no one knew what was going to happen or what the repercussions would be, all that could be surmised was that whatever was happening was bad news.

They remained unmoved throughout the afternoon as the news slowly came through. In London the House of Parliament had been destroyed as well as various other buildings of significance and the British people were now being ruled from a bunker that for security reasons could not have its location identified. It sounded like everything was turning to shit and if it hadn't been for the alien abductions the country would almost certainly have descended in to total chaos.

FORTY

It was the advent of night that immediately worried Clare and the realisation that Lisa was still out there somewhere, who knew where. The news from Russia was the same as that in Britain and whilst the area was a lot bigger it was still being reported that somewhere in the region of a hundred million people had been abducted from various sites in the vast country.

"I'm going to try and phone her," Clare declared picking up her phone. Jack's silence was read as a clear yes to the idea so Clare set about making the call.

"It's ringing," she announced, relaying what was happening to Jack who was by now deep in to a fresh bag of hashish. He somehow knew this was going to happen, the alien invasion, the mass abductions, everything. He had no idea how he'd come to this conclusion but he was sure.

"Jack ..." Clare's voice quivered as she handed the phone to him.

"Yes," he said looking up, sensing the fear and panic in her voice as he took the phone off her. He put the phone to his ear, what he heard he didn't understand and a look of serious worry appeared on his face. It looked like all the blood was draining from his face.

"What, what was it Jack?" Clare asked.

"I don't know but ... it didn't sound human did it?"

Jack's heavy session of hashish abuse suddenly

recoiled as worry and fear came to rule his mind.

"Do you think she's been taken?" Clare asked. Jack knew that she had gone but he didn't know how to tell Clare. Then it came to him, the noise on the other end of the phone was the same as when his phone had been stolen in London by the homeless street drinkers that fateful first night.

"She'll be fine, she'll be back with us soon," Jack said hoping to calm Clare's nerves.

"How do you know? We don't even know where she is, what's happened to her?"

Jack knew that nothing he could say would calm the situation and as usual his immediate response was to roll another joint; a real monster of a joint to take all the stress out of the dire situation. Less than an hour later and the pair of them were in bed asleep; the joint had worked its magic and sleep came easily.

~ ~ ~

The next morning Jack sat at the kitchen table trying to work out what exactly was going on. There was so much to consider; work being one of them, Lisa being another and that just covering the personal stuff. If Jack began thinking about the planetary situation he would really get drawn in to the quagmire. One bad development that had seemingly happened overnight was the end of TV transmissions. There were no news channels up and running so Jack went to look for his old analogue radio. Flicking it to long-wave he began scanning the frequencies and eventually he stumbled across something; the voice was definitely human but was not speaking English but Jack saw that at least there was some human control still in place somewhere. After a few more minutes an English voice began to talk.

"The alien force have come and taken our planet. They launched a full-scale invasion just before six a.m. GMT Monday and have taken people from all the main cities of Earth. If you are one of the few who have yet to surrender you should report to a re-conditioning centre details of which are available on any UK based news website. If you do not follow these instructions our new rulers have vowed to use terminal force."

Jack knew time was running out and went back to the bedroom where Clare still lay deep in sleep. He shook her awake and immediately that look of panic stared back at him.

"What?"

"We've got to get out otherwise we are really fucked," Jack announced hoping to cajole her out of bed.

"What? What's going on?"

"It's a full-scale planetary invasion, we've been told to go to some centre. It's for the best babe; we've got to get out and now!"

"Well if it's that bad I want one last thing off you," Clare countered.

"Yeah, what is it?"

"I think you know," she said lifting the duvet up to reveal her beautiful naked body. Within seconds Jack was on top of her, fucking fiercely as if his life depended on it. For all he knew maybe it did.

~ ~ ~

After checking the laptop for instructions as to where they had to go Jack and Clare left the flat, quite possibly

237

for the last time. They both sensed it would be some time before they could return; it was going to be a long, strange struggle to survive. The nearest 'reconditioning centre' was just outside of town fortunately but it seemed to Jack that it was the designation destination for a wide area around. The next nearest centre was in Southampton to the west and London to the north, there was nothing to the east.

Walking through the Brighton suburbs Jack and Clare became really aware of just how alone they really were. News must have reached a lot of the other survivors early and then to stop for that one last fuck had delayed them for a couple of extra hours. As they reached the university district there was no one around but the camp was now close. When they arrived it was clear they had been lied to, it was not a 'reconditioning centre' it was a battle station. A last chance for humanity to keep a grip on the planet they had inhabited. All of the centres were apparently like this and each knew that once the aliens came it would be a long and bloody fight. Jack and Clare were unsure what to do, should they stay and fight or could they just survive by themselves, on the road. Jack reckoned if they kept moving around they would be a lot safer that if they stayed at the centre where inevitably they would end up having to fight and who knew exactly how good the weapons provided would be able to kill the aliens. No one knew, they just assumed. Assumption was not something Jack wanted to rely on. Despite this they decided to spend the night at the centre. It was cold outside but here at the center they had bunk beds and heating and despite this as they both fell off to sleep that night they knew tomorrow they would be moving on. It was deep in to the night though when Clare had another idea.

Dear Jack,
I'm so very sorry to do this to you but I have a confession. I'm in love with Lisa and I must be with her so I've gone to look. I know she is out there somewhere, waiting for me and I know I must go and find her.
Clare.

The note he found by his bed that next morning sent him spiralling to a new low; how could she do this? He had seen it coming but with all that had happened in the previous thirty-six hours how could she pick now to go and find Lisa. He knew however that whatever the circumstances he needed to get out of the centre but where he wasn't sure. Should he follow Clare? The only problem was he had no idea where she was heading? Surely she couldn't be heading to Russia?

Jack decided to walk the Sussex countryside and see what was going on but as he started out he realised there was no one around. Jack knew what he needed to do. He found a car nearby, broke in to it and got behind the wheel. He'd never driven a car before but where he came from it was almost seen as part of any kid's education to learn how to break in to and hot-wire a car. The engine geared up and Jack headed north, towards London, towards home. There was nowhere else left for him to go, not now since Clare had left him.

FORTY-ONE

It took a few hours for Jack to get the car to the outer suburbs of London. Once he'd got the habit of which was the brake pedal and which was the accelerator he found the whole deal pretty straightforward. He simply left the car in second gear and moved forward; he never had any reason to reverse so it was easy to manoeuvre. It wasn't until he reached the suburb that used to be his home though it truly dawned on just how bad things had got in the city. He eventually stopped, rather than parked, the car outside Clare's old house on Elgin Close and got out. All the way down the high street lay bodies armed with various pieces of weaponry. Everyone was dead; he was the only person out on the street who was alive. He couldn't even imagine there was anyone in any of the houses that seemingly lay empty. He drove down to a nearby supermarket and was pleased to see that a lot of the fast food was still available. He filled the back seat of the car up with all kinds of food with long lives until their expiration date. It wasn't the healthiest stuff but right now Jack didn't care, all he wanted was food to keep him going. His next stop was work and as he again turned to head north he headed up the hill to Crystal Palace. As the car reached the peak he was presented with a new panoramic view of the city of London. There were buildings still ablaze and a lot of the newer building were just gone. It was a dreadful scene and Jack sat back for a while contemplating the scene of destruction before him.

'Shit,' he thought, 'what the hell can I do now? Where can I go?'

He had no answers, he had no idea where he could go or what he could do. It was then it dawned on him and immediately he knew where he needed to be and what he needed to be doing. He turned the car around and headed back south. He had a plan; he knew what he needed to do.

Driving back to Brighton was an easy exercise until he reached the suburbs where some vigilante groups, probably from the centre he'd spent his last night with Clare at, were roaming around. They were firing at anything in the sky but a few of them looked at Jack with quizzical eyes as if to ask what he was doing. He simply kept his head down and drove slowly through the area they had apparently seized control of.

Finally hitting the town centre Jack was delighted to see it was still pretty much as it had been when he'd left. Hardly any buildings had been destroyed and the only thing odd about the whole situation was the lack of people. He guessed most people had gone to the battle station. He dumped the car outside his drug dealers' house and broke in. It was easy and part one of his mission was complete once he'd found the stash of hashish that was always lying around.

Moving back to the car he loaded the supplies in to the back seat and again moved off this time in the direction of the old flat. Pulling up outside he grabbed a few bags of food and the huge bag of hashish and unlocked the front door. The house had clearly lay empty since Jack and Clare had made their get-away less than thirty-six hours earlier.

He walked up the stairs to the old top-floor flat where

he dumped most of the goods. He plugged in the kettle to brew some tea and was delighted to see that the electricity supply was still working. After the tea had been made he sat in his chair and proceeded to roll a joint. He had an awful lot to think about and he was pleased to have some time.

Work was fucked, his relationship was fucked, all his friends, all of his old friends anyway he simply assumed were dead and what did he have to live for. He turned on the TV and again there was no news, somewhat surreally the only channels that had continued to broadcast were the old, golden oldies. If you wanted to know what was going on you had no chance but if you wanted to watch I Love Lucy you were in heaven. Jack turned the TV off and plugged in his stereo. He knew what music he needed to listen too, there was no other choice. It had to be REM and the song had to be "It's The End of the World As We Know It." But unfortunately for Jack everything was not fine, everything was in fact at a new all-time low. Life would never be the same again. After a few joints and a few more records Jack felt doomed. There was nowhere for him to go, there was nothing he could do to improve his situation. With life now being all about survival there seemed very little point to it. He continued to smoke through his dealers' supply uncaring to how much he was using and unwilling to consider the implications.

That night he toiled in bed, unable to sleep even after all that hashish he'd smoked. Even worse were the thoughts that were beginning to dominate his mind, they were some very dark thoughts. When he woke the next morning he simply began to cry, sobbing like a little baby who needed his Mum. He hadn't cried like this for years, since his Grans' funeral, and he decided he needed some fresh air. Whenever he felt awful it was always good for him to get some air and right now he felt more awful than at any time in his life. It was a completely futile existence.

'What's the fucking point?' he thought as he descended the stairs. He smoked a large mostly hashish joint as he left the house. Standing on the front steps of the house he looked around, there was no one anywhere. He decided to go and look at the beach and sea and then it came to him.

'If life wasn't worth living, why bother?' It was with this in his mind that he walked over the road and on to the beach. He didn't stop, he just continued until he was in the water.

'This is it,' he thought as he felt the first wave crash over his head as he walked off in to the deep, deep sea. There was no point left to his life and this was the easiest way to end all those years of suffering. His life, as a member of the forgotten generation, had long been about suffering but now it was time to end it all.

It was then it happened, a lone UFO came in to view and with its tractor beam trapping him he was at once saved and captured. Now life really wouldn't be the same ever again ...

Thank you for reading.

Please review this book. Reviews help others find New Pulp Press and inspire us to keep providing these marvelous tales.

If you would like to be put on our email list to receive updates on new releases, contests, and promotions, please go to NewPulpPress.com and sign up.

Acknowledgement

I'd like to take this rare opportunity to acknowledge some people without whose support this would ever have happened. Thanks goes out to you too for buying this. My parents, with them anything is possible; Steve Williams at Dead Snakes, MH Clay and Johnny Olsen at the Mad Swirl and the gloriously deranged Ben John Smith at the magnificent Horror-Sleaze-Trash. Whenever I write fiction and I think it's getting out of control I just think of Ben and decide to push it all the way over the edge. Also, thanks to all my friends, especially those who have helped me out over the decades it has taken to get here.

About the Author

Bradford Middleton was born in the working-class suburbs of southeast London in 1971 and spent the next 30 years trying to escape. He now lives in Brighton and has been trying to escape here since about 2008. He has been published widely, with over 100 unique publications, at places like *Over My Dead Body!*, *Rolling Thunder Quarterly*, *Work Literary Magazine*, *Empty Mirror*, *Ppigpenn*, *Zygote in my Coffee*, *Mad Swirl*, *Horror-Sleaze-Trash*, *Fuck Fiction*, *Dead Snakes* and Camel Saloon. In 2013 he won the inaugural Twitter fiction competition from Brighton Fringe Festival, and the following year won the Twitter slam at the Brighton Digital Festival. Last year he gladly finished his debut novel DIVE which he is pretty sure will drive everyone insane! Want to read his award-winning tweets or just follow the general madness of his life then head over to @beatnikbraduk.

NewPulpPress.com

www.ingramcontent.com/pod-product-compliance
Lightning Source LLC
Chambersburg PA
CBHW060544260626
47161CB00003B/1042